Typically
TANYA

Taha Kehar is a Karachi-based journalist. He's written for both Indian and Pakistani magazines, newspapers and publications. He's the author of a novel titled Of Rift and Rivalry. *Typically Tanya* is his second work of fiction.

TAHA KEHAR

Typically
TANYA

HarperCollins *Publishers* India

First published in India by
HarperCollins *Publishers* in 2018
A-75, Sector 57, Noida, Uttar Pradesh 201301, India
www.harpercollins.co.in

2 4 6 8 10 9 7 5 3 1

P-ISBN: 978-93-5302-345-4
E-ISBN: 978-93-5302-346-1

Typeset in 11/14 Sabon LT Std at
Manipal Digital Systems, Manipal

Printed and bound at
Thomson Press (India) Ltd

For Anaa, who saw it all,
and
for Pashi and Naz, who made sure that I did too.

O Captain, my Careem

I sink my elbow into a sofa cushion, heave a long sigh and ransack my bag in a frantic search for my cell phone. My hand scoops up a slim eye pencil and an empty bottle of lip gloss. I plunge them back into the bag – it's one of those cavernous carpet ones from Khaadi – and continue rummaging, unwilling to accept defeat.

After a seemingly endless struggle, I find my phone tucked under crumpled receipts, a lipstick, a compact mirror and a deodorant. I pluck it out and hurriedly attempt to book a Careem cab. As I lean back on the sofa and sip a steaming cup of tea, a small circle spins on the phone's screen. It's moving slowly, as if my phone considers booking a cab a trivial command that it would rather ignore.

'Ugh,' I murmur. 'I'll be late for work again today.'

I can see Mummy ambling down the staircase. Her hips jiggle and bounce from one side to the other and her heels click against the marble floor. She looks like a belly dancer who is out of practice. As she descends the last few steps, she tosses her head back, flips her hennaed hair over her shoulder and ties it into a messy fishtail braid. I rise to my feet and hook my bag onto my arm to create the illusion of composure. I don't want Mummy thinking that I'm dawdling at home, or getting worked up at the slightest provocation. After all, I'm nothing like her.

'Tanya, are you going to work?' Mummy asks as she plops herself on the sofa.

'No, I'm playing *chupan chupayee* with the Careem Captain,' I say, looking at my phone, hoping for a miracle. 'You can never trust these Careem chauffeurs to show up anywhere on time.'

'Are you sure it's safe to travel in a Careem, *beta*?' Mummy tucks a stray strand of hair behind her ear. 'Why don't you take my car? Saira has told me so many horror stories about Careem drivers. They've become a nightmare for passengers! Nighat was complaining about some Pathan driver who abandoned her and a bunch of her friends on Shahrah-e-Faisal at night. They were near PAF Museum and had to walk all the way to Lal Qila restaurant until they could find a ride home. *Uff*, just thinking about it gives me goosebumps.'

'Mummy, please!' Annoyance creeps into my voice. 'It's completely safe.'

She waves a hand in the air, averts her gaze and shrugs.

'And to be honest,' I say through clenched teeth, 'Nighat is known to be a bit vicious. She probably made a snarky comment about how the driver's kameez didn't match his shalwar. That probably pissed him off.'

'Don't say that about poor Niggi,' Mummy clicks her tongue and glares at me as if I'd insulted her own child. 'Saira says her baby is an innocent victim everyone keeps picking on these days. *Bechari*.'

'Maybe if she didn't flaunt her daddy's money, I'd respect her more,' I quip as I make another attempt to book a Careem.

'*Khair*,' Mummy says. 'All I'm saying is that you should be careful when travelling with these drivers.'

Although Mummy's anxieties often irritate me, I've learnt, for obviously selfish reasons, not to ignore all of them. Getting into a car with a stranger is a dangerous prospect in these hapless times. And I certainly wouldn't go to the extent of saying that peace has been restored in Karachi, though Operation Lyari of 2013, to quell gang violence and the Nine Zero raid, carried out to clip the Muttahida Qaumi Movement's (MQM) wings were attempts to ensure this. The authorities may have done a good job in making some deluded citizens believe that the city has become safer, now that the MQM years are behind us, but Mummy and I are not that easy to convince. As long as Mummy's solitaires continue to be stolen at gunpoint when she travels to a *shaadi* and Altaf Bhai continues to make hate speeches, there's no point in the Pakistan Rangers extending their powers to purge the city of troublemakers.

'You're probably right, Mummy,' I say as I place my phone on the coffee table and smile at her. 'I'm sick of using my phone to book cabs that take me from Defence to Burns Road just because I can afford to do so. If you ask me, I prefer travelling in a rickshaw, with the breeze and dust flying into my hair and the sun warming my skin.'

Mummy's eyes widen with disbelief. I know that a new fear has sprung in her heart.

'If I ever see you getting into a rickshaw, I'll scream till my lungs burst,' she wags her finger at me. 'Your skin will turn dark and your hair will lose its shine!'

I nod, even though I find her reasons quite absurd. If I don't agree with Mummy, she will continue arguing in an increasingly shrill, piercing voice, and I'm already sleep-deprived. I don't have the stamina for a screaming match.

Besides, her fears have a measure of truth to them. Why shouldn't I be scared of a rickshaw-wallah or even a strange Careem chauffeur? I wouldn't want to be bludgeoned with an axe by an average desi Joe, if not by a war-mongering militant as most people would expect. If I'm lucky enough to survive, I'd probably have to spend a fortune on reconstructive surgery. Even though Mummy knows a world-class plastic surgeon at South City Hospital, he isn't in the business of giving discounts like a stall owner at the bustling Juma Bazar on Johar Mor. It is difficult to fritter away your hard-earned money on such extravagances.

And anyway, after exhausting all my rather limited options, I'd have to borrow from Mummy – and that would only open the floodgates to an entire bucketful of complaints. Quite frankly, even World Bank loans to exploit cash-strapped nations come with fewer conditions than a handout from Mummy to me.

'Mummy,' I sit next to her on the sofa and hold her in a warm, purposeful embrace. 'May I borrow a thousand rupees? My salary is late again this month. I'll pay you back as soon as I get paid...'

Mummy nods and reaches for her purse. I close my eyes and pray that she takes out the right amount from her wallet. Ever since she spotted the first grey hair on her scalp, Mummy started losing her memory. Her eyesight is also getting weaker and this supposed folly of old age has not been working to my advantage.

The last time I asked her for a thousand rupees, she'd handed me five crumpled twenty-rupee notes and promptly walked away, depriving me of the opportunity to tell her about the error. If she repeats this mistake, I'll have to start carrying a begging bowl and badger her for money. If that doesn't work, I'll send her to Edhi Home where she can spend her twilight years in a comfortable place that is many, many miles away from me.

'There you go, *beta*,' she says, closing her purse with a sense of finality and holding out a crisp note. 'Thousand rupees for my *gareeb*, starving daughter. Enjoy.'

My mother knows how to do favours for people and then embarrass them by bringing it up in bizarre ways. Fortunately, Mummy's eyesight hasn't failed her this time, so I don't complain. As I happily place the note in my wallet, I contemplate the possibility of ordering a roast beef burger from Hanifia on Boat Basin and drinking kahwa from Dera. It's always the small needs that matter the most when your salary has been delayed and there isn't even a paisa that you can call your own.

3 p.m.

The muggy air thickens in the living room. The ceiling fan clicks and hums above my head as it draws away the heat. A few seconds later, it stops spinning and silence fills the air.

'Not again,' I groan.

As I say these words, the whirr of our generator rips through the stillness. Haji, Mummy's loyal man Friday – whom I call Lurch because he has lousy housekeeping skills like the servant in *The Addams Family* and an unalloyed loyalty to my mother – is the only one in the house who knows how to switch the generator on. But in other matters of housework, Mummy's training has given him zero skills. What more can I expect from my mother? Mummy, who has returned to her room to shower for the sixth time today, probably hasn't noticed that the electricity has gone. She won't realize it until the chill of the air-conditioning dissipates from her room.

By the time the fan turns on again and I've messaged K-Electric on 8119 about the power breakdown, I've made myself a chilled glass of lime juice. But the app is still struggling to find me a 'Captain'. In half an hour, I've found and lost three drivers already. Two of those drivers accepted my ride request and refused to turn up when they couldn't find the place. God, I have never had this much bad luck with an app. I didn't even swipe left as many times as this when I was briefly on Tinder.

I recline against a backrest pillow and try once again. My mind shifts towards the fear of being axed to death by a stranger. I guess I have some insecurities about travelling in a Careem. It's mostly to do with the fact that I am one of those sheltered journalists. You know, the ones who hide behind their desks editing stories – cleaning and polishing them like they're a pair of mud-stained boots – instead of venturing out on hardcore assignments like their colleagues. It's a difficult position to be in when you dream about being on the other side, hunting for stories rather than inserting commas and full-stops in the right places to make a messy sentence glimmer with purpose.

The hum of my ringtone disrupts my thoughts. It's Topsy – my thirty-something lawyer friend Tabassum. I plug in my headphones and answer the phone.

'Hey babe, are you at work?'

'Umm, I'm trying to get there,' I say, sounding defeated. 'The bloody Careem app is acting up. Oh well, what's been up?'

'I have to tell you something,' Topsy says, with a throb of impatience in her voice. 'Bilal flew down from Lahore yesterday. And last night, he tried something ... well ... something I've never really done before.'

'*Aha*, give me the juicy details,' I say, feigning interest while returning to the Careem app.

'So ... he's got whips lying around in his closet,' Topsy giggles. 'He told me if I am a good girl, he won't use them on me. That gave me an incentive to be bad. Very bad. So we basically whipped each other all through the night and made wild, lustful love.'

As she narrates her tale of bondage and sadomasochism, Topsy giggles softly like a teenager.

'Easy there, tigress,' I place my phone on the table, thrilled at having found a Careem driver mere minutes into the call. 'You never know when that whip turns into an axe.'

She cackles loudly and the image of the simpering teenager dissipates from my mind.

'But it's good that you're taking a walk on the dark side,' I say. 'How did that tame, lovesick divorcee I met all those years ago turn into this relentless nymphomaniac?'

'What can I say, darling?' Topsy says, though not without pride. 'Men take to me with ease.'

'It's another thing altogether that they eventually find themselves in a pool of Absolut Vodka and a bed with crumpled sheets.'

'Ha-ha-ha. But to answer your question, it's all because of Bilal. He has brought my darkest fantasies and fetishes out in the open. At times, his eagerness to do strange things surprises me.'

'That's okay,' I reassure her. 'Sometimes you need someone who can broaden your perspective. You know, so you can make space for all the *new* fetishes that you pick up along the way.'

Topsy has never needed an excuse to tell me about how much action she's been getting. After going through an acrimonious divorce two years ago, she had trapped herself in a shell of self-pity and shame. During that period, her apartment in Clifton was a museum to the memories she shared with her ex-husband, Khalid, who had walked out on her for a younger, kinkier woman.

From the Gulgee paintings that hung on the walls to the china that was stored in her kitchen cabinets, everything reminded her of Khalid. Back then, Topsy was docile and reserved. She reminded me, in many ways, of a younger version of Mummy after Daddy had left her. The only difference was that Topsy had a string of secret affairs to fill the vacuum and prevent loneliness from becoming her sole companion.

Since meeting Bilal, Topsy has become more open about the men she is passionate about. Her stories are met with raised eyebrows, stunned silences and backbiting from the *fundoo* brigade. But I doubt she cares about people's reactions.

'*Waise,* if you think about it, I've been with all sorts of men who derive pleasure from being my muse and passion,' she says, fishing for compliments and a little attention.

'Certainly,' I reply, taking a sip of lime juice. 'My favourites among your men are the ones who end up marrying women who lurk through the moonlit streets of Saddar Bazaar in shuttlecock burqas.'

'Please, I've done better than that,' Topsy laughs.

'Yes, of course. How can I forget the other variety? You know, the ones who are destined to tie the knot with "modren" women with lacquered faces who are seen window-shopping at Dolmen Mall.'

'What can I say?' she giggles. 'The Clifton Bridge doesn't stop me from meeting men from the other side.'

'I must admit, Topsy, this Lahori hunk you share a bed with these days is quite unlike the lousy Romeos and sex-deprived *aashiq*s you've attracted in the past.'

'What can I say, Punjabi men have a wild streak,' she whispers.

'Sadly, the only men who come to see me are Careem Captains. Which reminds me, I should go see where my Captain is. I'm already running late.'

As I hang up, I notice the Captain's name on the app – Bakhtullah Khan. I'll call him Bakhtu Bhai, just in case he gets any ideas.

My GPS tells me he's near Abdullah Shah Ghazi's Mausoleum. It's only a few minutes away from our sprawling, dust-infested house on E Street. Bakhtu Bhai should be able to find it easily. It's close to Nabila's salon, Ensemble and the pricey restaurants where the rich, famous and the pointless regularly dine. I guess that's why Mummy is so reluctant to move to another neighbourhood.

3.12 p.m.

I rummage through my bag, pluck out a ballpoint pen and a notepad and scribble out a list of story ideas I want to work on at the *Daily Image* that Hassan – my cranky, overbearing city editor with a weakness for eye candy – probably won't let me work on. As the seconds tick away into minutes, I tear out the page and toss it into the bin. What's the point? The app shows me that my Captain is outside the wrought-iron gates of the house. I'm glad that Bakhtu Bhai has arrived at his destination without the usual *nakhre* of his colleagues. Will Tanya Shaukat give her Captain a five-star rating today?

Lurch comes into the room to inform me about a white Corolla parked outside.

His brisk, ungainly sprint from the kitchen to the living room makes my heart pound like a sledgehammer. Why do Mummy's hired help have to be so needlessly hyper in their quest to prove how efficient they can be?

'*Gaadi aayi hai,* baby,' he says, gasping for breath.

I still don't understand why he insists on calling me 'baby'. I guess it's a term of endearment, suffused with the warmth and respect he feels towards my mother. After all, Mummy's servants wouldn't care about me had it not been for their twisted, pseudo-umbilical connection with her.

'The app has already told me, you silly man,' I roll my eyes and whisper to myself as I clutch my bag and run to the door. I smile politely at Lurch so he doesn't think I'm being rude.

3.25 p.m.

I hop into the Corolla and don my Ray-Bans. A mid-afternoon Karachi sun stalks me as I shut the door, its punishing rays licking the skin on my hands. I click my tongue. Bakhtu Bhai turns around, nods and whispers a polite salaam.

'*Garmi hai na,* Madam?' he says, stating the obvious with a saber-toothed smile that fills me with unease. Ignoring his comment, I wave my hand in the air and point towards the AC vent. He flicks the button on the dashboard and starts the engine.

For the first few minutes, the whiff of coconut oil merges with the mildewed stench of the AC. Between the blazing heat and the malodorous smell, I don't know which to blame more for my discomfort.

My friends have often told me stories of meaningful conversations they have struck up with Careem chauffeurs. I wonder if Bakhtu Bhai will open new doors and windows for me to advance my career prospects. My friend Sonia, a health reporter at the *Daily Image*, once based a story on the brother of one of her Careem Captains. His gall bladder surgery was botched up by doctors at a local hospital and he had scars to prove that a kidney racket was operating at the facility.

But Sonia isn't a topnotch reporter and her story lacked research and insight. After the story was published, her Careem driver's brother professed that he had lied to the media. A few days later, the unfortunate patient held a press conference where he revealed that he was an absconding member of Uzair Baloch's gang from Lyari. He had fallen out of the gangster's favour and been roughed up by his old cronies. He wanted to use the story published in the *Daily Image* as a means of approaching the media without eliciting suspicion so he could expose his old friends.

The newspaper ran a corrigendum to put an end to this fiasco and prevent the hospital from suing the reporter who published the story. On her part, Sonia didn't bother to explain her position. What more can one expect from a self-styled, Armani-clad journalist with no real interest in the grassroots?

At least we sub-editors are good at what we do, even though we don't get to go to an MQM rally near Water Pump or smoke smelly bidis with a bus driver from Bajaur Agency. Such possibilities have anyway always made Mummy anxious. She thinks I'll get smashed to smithereens in a bomb blast. Either way, I'm beginning to enjoy the stress, ambiguities and challenges that come with being a sub. There's always the chance of a silent explosion triggered by an unwanted error on the pages or a cluttered news report that finds its way to my inbox. Who needs to be in the field when the drama can crawl into the newsroom and make itself comfortable on the dusty revolving chairs of our workstations?

3.35 p.m.

Ten minutes into the cab ride, I realize that unlike his colleagues, the bearded and burly Bakhtu Bhai will not be able to give me any insights. And we haven't even reached Sunset Boulevard yet. I wonder how I will make it through the rest of the journey. I'm not saying this because I'm afraid. The truth is, all he seems keen on is picking his nose and burping. 'Where are you from?' I ask him, interrupting a particularly intense dig and cringing at how pretentious my Urdu accent sounds.

'Bannu,' he says, rather hesitantly. '*Bohat achi jaga haiwoh.*'

'Yes, of course,' I reply, my voice dripping with unintended sarcasm. 'Bannu is amazing.'

Bakhtu Bhai senses my scepticism and decides to remain quiet for the rest of the ride. I wonder if he's carrying an axe in the boot. The Rangers may have managed to sideline some of those dubious elements that lurked the streets of my city, but what if Bakhtu Bhai is actually one of those gangsters like in those Bollywood movies Mummy loves? Worse, what if he's a militant who escaped the tribal areas after the Operation?

At this point, Bakhtu Bhai pulls over outside my office – he seems to have taken a shortcut because I always get stuck near Kala Pul for twenty minutes every day. I hand him a bundle of paan-stained notes and smile.

'*Shukriya, beti,*' he says.

I wonder what he's thanking me for? I did take a swipe at his hometown. I watch silently as my Captain's Corolla turns towards the main road. As it moves past the office building, I hear something rattling in the boot.

Maybe he did want to bludgeon me to death after all. God bless these stereotypes about war-mongering Pukhtuns from the tribal belt who carry arms like they're umbrellas or car keys. If not for these convenient notions, I wouldn't have a scapegoat in Bakhtu Bhai.

I wouldn't blame him for wanting to kill me. Many people want to see Tanya Shaukat on the guillotine.

Braham and the Other Daghs

7 September 2016

3.45 p.m.

'There's something about this Brahamdagh Bugti that I find unsettling,' Hafeez tells a stocky, bespectacled man with a thick beard who is sitting next to him on a bench in the smoking area, then takes a drag of his cigarette. The man nods with robotic sternness, yawns audibly and stubs his cigarette on the bench.

'Are you referring to his bewitching eyes or receding hairline,' I walk over to Hafeez and pull out a cigarette from a pack of Marlboro Lights.

The bearded man looks at me, rubs his elbow as if to excuse himself from the conversation and turns away.

'All I'm saying is,' Hafeez smiles at me and rises from the bench, 'how does a vile, virile Baloch man strike up a convenient arrangement and gain political asylum? The whole fiasco seems a little fishy, if you ask me.'

'You said the same about Kulbhushan Jadhav,' I say, derision piercing my voice as I light my cigarette. 'I get it already. Enough with your conspiracy theories.'

'*Nahin* yaar, the biggest game is being played in Kashmir,' Hafeez chips in with enthusiasm. 'I was just editing this story on the violence happening there. People are being blinded with pellet guns! It's just cruel.'

'So what do you get from talking about it?'

'Nothing, just the satisfaction of talking about it,' he holds out his hands in the sticky September air. 'I'm a journalist after all. I'm entitled to a rigid opinion that gets me into trouble.'

Although he's my closest friend at work, I find it difficult to understand Hafeez's inflexible opinions on political events. He is a conspiracy theorist with the heart of a jingoistic warrior. His view on everything – from the Kashmir issue to the Panama leaks – are coloured with his tedious brand of patriotism. I enjoy his company, especially because of his tight-fitted blue jeans that accentuate his 'posterior. If only Hafeez paid more attention to his shirts, we could take our unspoken infatuation for each other to the next level. Until that time comes, my feelings for him will probably continue to drift between various extremes, unmoored by intimacy.

'You're in earlier than usual, *kya aaj Eid hai?* Or has the journalist in you returned from hibernation?'

It's typical of Hafeez to make an acidic remark to draw attention to himself. Can't he say hello like a normal person?

'Hardly a journalist, *meri jaan*,' I reply, stubbing my cigarette against a green bench. 'Editors aren't journalists. They work backstage and live vicariously.'

'You and living vicariously?' Hafeez points a finger at me and laughs.

'Screw you, you know exactly what I'm talking about.' The pitch of my voice may have gone up a few decibels because the man Hafeez was speaking to turns around, shoots a deadpan look at us and returns to his second cigarette.

'*Chhodo* yaar, tell me, are you going to Sonia's wedding bash tonight?' Hafeez asks.

'Shit, I completely forgot,' my words slip out surreptitiously, almost in a whisper.

'Well, you should remember already. I spoke to her yesterday and she's looking forward to seeing you at the wedding.'

'But why?' I screech. The bespectacled man turns again but doesn't have the guts to look directly at me.

'Don't be silly, she wants you there,' Hafeez says in an attempt to reason with me. 'Forget whatever happened.'

But I can't. Everyone expects me to explain how I ended up sleeping with Sonia's fiancé, even though it was many months ago and I was drunk. Not as drunk or high as Topsy is when she contemplates having sex with a stranger, but drunk enough to make the mistake of sleeping with the fiancé of the soft-spoken yet abrasive health reporter who unearths stories through Careem Captains and throws dull wedding bashes that people like me forget about.

'Do you think I'm the one being bitter?' I snap at him. 'Okay, maybe a little. But everyone knows that Saad — that cheating, low-life, scum-of-a-fiancé of hers — came on to me.'

'I understand, T,' his soft voice soothes me. 'But why get into all this right now? She's marrying him.'

'Trust me, Hafeez, the morning after the deed was done, I wanted to tell Sonia everything,' I hear myself say, and I'm shocked by my own honesty. 'It wasn't worth it to keep what happened a secret. And the sex was terrible. But Saad stopped me and insisted that we keep it hidden.'

'So why did you listen to him?' Hafeez asks. Hafeez might sound like he knows nothing, but he's heard this story a million times. He still insists on hearing it again, like a child who falls asleep to the same bedtime story every night.

'Well, we mutually agreed not to tell her anything until we'd discussed it beforehand. However, Saad defied our pact. He spilled out the details of what happened that night and distorted them to make it sound like it was all my fault. Sonia believed every word he said without hearing my version of the story.'

'I get why you were so bummed out by what she said,' Hafeez says and then lights another cigarette.

'Hah, when I tried to reason with her, she said that she wouldn't expect any less from the daughter of a man who left his wife.'

'Ouch.'

'Everything changed with those words, Hafeez,' I rise from the bench and toss my stub into a bin. 'And really, isn't a girl allowed at least one mistake? Anyway, what will I achieve by being stern with myself when the so called "good ones" are stooping low enough to insult my lineage?'

'But you wouldn't approve of a friend sleeping with your fiancé, would you? If not, then you're a hypocrite.'

'Does that count as hypocrisy?' I say as I walk out of the smoking area. 'Maybe. But if I'm a hypocrite, Sonia is, at the least, an idiot.'

'That's why you have me to balance the both of you out.' Hafeez adjusts the collar of his shirt and follows me to our work station.

'Where would we be without you, Hafeez?' I say, only half sarcastic. '*Waise*, it's been months since Sonia and I started talking again. But I still think she shouldn't be marrying Saad. Topsy tells me he's seeing her sister Mehnaz – or Mopsy as they call her.'

'Ha-ha, poor Mopsy is the light and easy broccoli salad that Saad will have with his steak.' Hafeez holds the door open for me.

'I'd be deeply offended if anyone referred to me as an easy broccoli salad.' I push him in through the door. 'I don't get why Sonia doesn't so much as listen to me about Mopsy.'

'All these Mopsys can be easily mopped away, Tanya,' Hafeez imitates Sonia, capturing the Sindhi twang of her accent to perfection.

'And you know how I'd mop them away,' I pitch in with a throatier impersonation of Sonia.

A sinister smile appears on Hafeez's face. I look into his eyes for a little longer than I should, clear my throat and look away.

'You know, Sonia could use a poke every now and then to ease the strain on her heart and mind,' I say.

'After tonight, she'll be getting more than the occasional poke,' Hafeez sniggers.

'I'm not referring to sex.' I place my hands on my hips in mock protest. 'How crass of you to assume that! I was referring to a genuinely painful poke. Seriously, I'm not kidding, yaar.'

'Sure, T, I believe you.'

'What sort of woman do you think I am? My friend might have turned on me for a bloodthirsty, egotistical savage, but I'd never say such a thing about her! Ugh, Hafeez. Now I'm visualizing it. I didn't need a mental image.'

'I'm doing you a favour,' he says. 'That image will distract you when you meet Hassan. He's back from his trip to London.'

'Is that right?' I respond nonchalantly. 'I wonder what his mistress had to say about Lun-dun.'

'Come on now, don't jump to conclusions,' Hafeez clicks his tongue. 'You always do that. In any case, I don't think it's a coincidence that Khirad and Hassan went on leave at the same time.'

'The woman sits next to me,' I whisper as we enter the newsroom. 'I know exactly what she's capable of. And frankly, she's totally his type.'

'Anyway,' Hafeez says irritably, conveying his disapproval about the direction of the conversation, 'Hassan came looking for you. He said it's important.'

'I doubt it is,' I place the pack of Marlboro Lights on my desk. 'He probably wants one of his girlfriends to be featured in the paper.'

4.15 p.m.

When I walk towards Hassan's musty office, Khirad is perched upon one corner of his desk. Clad in a red kurti, white pants, and heels that are high enough to kill her toes and break her ankles, she laughs while Hassan grabs her hand and gives it a mild pull.

The growing camaraderie between them makes me flinch with disgust. I knock on the glass panel door to his office, which has been carelessly left ajar. Khirad leaps from the desk like a frog and lands on the chair next to the table. Hassan coughs, lowers his gaze and waves his hand at me to tell me to enter.

His reaction is driven by fear. Mummy is friends with Hassan's wife, Bina. Ironically enough, she gives Bina advice on how to prevent her husband from having affairs. Believe it or not, one of Mummy's strategies is to encourage Bina to sing A. Nayyar's 'Bina tera naam' to Hassan every day so he remembers her name and doesn't even think about another woman. Are the lyrics flowing through Hassan's mind as I walk in? Does he think I'll tell my mother about his affair?

'Hi, Hassan,' I stifle the urge to giggle. There is a lilt in my voice that makes him sweat in terror. I look at Hassan and then at Khirad as they stare wordlessly at me.

'How was your vacation?' I ask, without realizing the implications of not speaking in the plural. The official story, my newswriting professor had taught me, has a truth of its own and should not be refuted, no matter what you hear through the grapevine.

'It was lovely,' Hassan turns to Khirad. She shoots a confused look at him. He twitches his brows and nods gently at her. Comprehension dawns on her face a few seconds later. She swivels her chair to face me and smiles in a restrained way.

'Oh yes, mine was also brilliant,' she feigns enthusiasm to conceal her ignorance. 'I just loved Lund ... Lahore summer.'

'Lahore summer?' I stare mutely at her as the words tumble out of my mouth. 'You're in the minority, I guess.'

'Yes ... well ... it's hot ... might as well get used to the tropics after ... umm.'

'Anyway,' Hassan interrupts, realizing Khirad's inability to sustain her lie. 'I've called both of you here because I need you to attend a conference today at the Arts Council. A British educationist will be there. Both of you have to cover the conference together. It'll go with a joint byline.'

I suppose I've got my byline for tomorrow. I wish it were for a story that I wanted to do and for which I wouldn't have to share the credit with Khirad. Her copy is an editor's nightmare. When she dies, she'll go straight to reporters' hell, where she belongs, for filing such god-awful copies.

'The event's in an hour,' Hassan says. 'Off you go. Also, Tanya Bibi, good edit on yesterday's lede.'

'Thanks,' I smile, slightly taken aback. It's rare that Hassan actually gives praise to people who aren't Khirad.

'But learn how to play to the gallery, Tanya,' he adds. 'Let yourself loose by using idioms.'

He sips his tea and starts gorging on a samosa that has been left on his desk by one of the chai-wallahs who lurk the corridors of our office.

God, I wish I could stuff those idioms up his behind so he could learn a thing or two about being a pain in the ass. I wonder who made a man like Hassan a city editor. All he does is fixate on idioms and womanize.

If you go by Hassan's book, journalism is as dirty as bad writing and cheap sex. Nothing makes a difference to him. As long as Khirad continues to take trips with him and the newspaper is replete with idioms, his full head of hair and ego will remain in its place. Maybe I should advise Mummy to tell Bina Hassan the story of Samson and Delilah. Now that's the kind of love which can make Hassan crawl on his knees and plead with Bina for forgiveness ... and probably lead to a wild night under their *razai*.

Chai pe Charchay

4.45 p.m.

After leaving Hassan's office, Khirad and I book a Careem for the event. Since I have to make it to Sonia's wedding bash at a respectable hour, which is any time after 11 p.m., I tell Khirad to take her laptop along so we can file the story from the venue.

I'm in no mood to get stuck in traffic during rush hour – especially not in a city like Karachi where driving comes with a death wish and accidents often leave you with more than just broken bones. Unfortunately, the Careem Captain – who is nothing like Bakhtu Bhai – starts to take the Shahrah-e-Faisal road during peak hours, when migraines are handed out as souvenirs after a long, tedious day.

'Why are you taking us through Shahrah-e-Faisal?' I protest to the Captain. 'Do you think we just moved to the city? Are you trying to get us to pay more by taking us via a longer route?'

'*Baji*, I'm taking you through the right route,' he replies glibly, as if he had anticipated my outburst and knows how to quell it.

'*Arre, bhai*,' I say, impatience growing within me. '*Ye kya baat hui?* I'm telling you what route to take us through and you insist on doing things your way!'

The Captain scoffs and accelerates the car past a fleet of Suzuki vans and an ornate bus that's wobbling down the road, leading us towards Qayyumabad Chowrangi.

'Let it be, Tanya,' Khirad gently pats my knee and turns towards the Captain. '*Bhai*, take us through whatever route you think best.'

The driver smiles at Khirad through the rearview mirror and averts his eyes when he catches me glaring at him.

I tell you, I'm jinxed. Nothing good will ever come out of my wishing for the finer things in life when people keep holding me back.

As we continue our journey at the mercy of our driver's rat-like navigation skills, Khirad speaks about her holiday and stutters each time the name of her actual vacation spot slips in at the wrong time. She compensates for these blunders by making references to Lahore's oppressive heat.

'So, what's the conference about?' I ask Khirad in an attempt to bring her out of her vacation mode.

'It's got something to do with education.'

'Yeah, I figured as much,' I say, a sliver of sarcasm settling into my tone. 'But who is this British educationist anyway and why is he speaking to the media?'

'Alan Trump. He's one of those foreigners who have come to reform the education system or something ... make it more English.'

'I thought the British left in 1947,' I quip.

'The *angrez* are great people ...' Khirad says primly. 'During my trip to Lund ... Lahore ... ah yes, the trip was excellent. How far are we?'

Khirad smiles and I don't mention her suspicious change of topic. We fall silent as we pass through a sea of traffic near Mövenpick Hotel. I scavenge through my bag and take out a lipstick and a small mirror to do a quick touch-up.

'I wonder if this post-colonial missionary will be tall and handsome,' I say, placing the mirror back into my bag.

'Are you looking for something serious?' Khirad asks, a smile flooding her face.

'Hell, no,' I retort. 'I'm just shopping around.'

Khirad gives a grunting laugh. I roll my eyes and look away. Why shouldn't I shop around? If Sonia can marry a flirt and Khirad can fool around with her boss, why should I be left behind? It's not like I'm hunting for Mr Right Now by using someone else's credit card. It would be best if people learnt to mind their own business. After the conference, I'll convince Alan Trump to make it mandatory for students to learn this skill at school.

5.15 p.m.

There's something about Alan Trump's speech that irks me. It has a strange, somnolent quality that leaves me feeling restless yet bored.

'All I want is for private education institutes in Pakistan to understand the importance of English,' the drone of his voice rings through the conference hall. 'If they don't teach children the language, most of the deserving ones – who end up at British universities – will struggle with English. This will interfere with their coursework.'

Alan needs a map to remind him which country he's in. Which 'deserving students' from Pakistan end up at British universities? The ones whose parents have huge pockets and seven cars?

I guess I'm being unfair to the poor chap though. It's probably the ambience that is making me doubt him all the more. I've never liked going to Arts Council – I find its architecture dull and uninspiring, and this forces me to find faults in what people say or do. If only Alan had the good sense to hold this event at NAPA, a three-minute walk away, I would have lost myself in the grandeur of the old Hindu Gymkhana building and perhaps taken a different view of his words. Even Mohatta Palace would have done the trick – a gentle sea breeze has an almost orgasmic effect on me. Or if he truly wanted me to enjoy the conference, he should have organized it at T2F. I'd happily sit through the entire event to honour the space Sabeen Mahmud gifted to Karachi.

But at the rate he's going, Alan Trump could run for president and still no one would listen. I bet he could give Donald a run for his money, though. I don't want a byline for this crap. If I put my name on this story, everyone will think that Tanya Shaukat is a *biki hui* journalist with a penchant for white men with no brains.

'The man is talking utter crap,' Khirad says , as if reading my mind. 'I'll file a small brief about this later. Let's get out of here.'

5.20 p.m.

We navigate our way through the crowd of TV cameramen and journalists scribbling away in their notebooks.

'Let's go get some chai,' Khirad says as we look for a Careem. 'Chai Wala, maybe?'

'Sure, let's go to a dhaba with our Fendi bags and throw out the chai-wallah and the original dhaba-goers while we're at it,' I respond wryly.

Khirad eyes me quizzically. She doesn't know I'm completely against the new trend of roadside tea establishments for the upper middleclass. It's just a phase, Tanya. It's just a bloody phase. I should stop my tirades against this phenomenon, at least when I'm in public. I turn away in embarrassment and change the topic.

'I've been craving the "Nutella paratha" served hot,' I say. 'Though Mummy says if I continue eating them, I'll explode. The woman thinks that all I need to catch an eligible boy is a slim figure.'

'My mother says the same things to me,' Khirad guffaws. 'She keeps taking me to *rishta* aunties.'

'Mummy is much too classy to opt for a *rishta* aunty,' I say, regretting the words as they fall out of my mouth – they make me sound cocky and elitist. 'She just can't handle these women who run matchmaking businesses on the telephone throughout the day. Unless it's during lunch or dinner-time and they're force-feeding their gigantic families *achaar gosht*,' I add, trying to take the sting out of my words.

Khirad doubles over with laughter and pats me on the back. I smile politely, surprised by her oafish reaction.

'My mother has also learnt a thing or two from my sister's experience,' she says, regaining composure.

'Did the *rishta* aunty parade your sister about only for her to be rejected by lecherous men and their mothers?'

'That's just one of the things that aunty did,' Khirad says as our Careem arrives and we get in. 'She lumped my sister into something called the "B-category" because she was slightly chubby. She then found fat old men from the same category for her.'

'I guess that's the easiest way to match-make, since there's no guarantee that opposites attract,' I say as I slam the car's door shut.

The Captain revs his engine and zooms past Zainab Market. As we drive towards Defence, I remember the time that Mummy confiscated a packet of crisps from my room.

'Do you want to be treated like a blob of fat that nobody wants, Tanya?' she had said. Even rhetorical questions bear the unquenchable thirst for answers when they're uttered in Mummy's voice. It's part of her allure. She's one to talk, really. I'm not the one who has pakoras every evening to go with my three cups of masala chai.

6 p.m.

The Captain turns into a congested street on Khayaban-e-Bukhari. It is teeming with kurta-clad men emerging out of Land Cruisers and making their way to the roadside dhaba. A bevy of security guards trail behind them.

'These men will never realize that you can't substitute a small dick with a big car,' I say without much thought. Khirad turns to me, her eyes widening with shock at my crass remark.

'I once dated a man who had a big Land Cruiser,' I add. 'Danish – I think that's what his name was. Now, *his* problem was that he had a security guard with him each time he picked me up from my house for a drive along Seaview.'

'Why would he do that?' Khirad chuckles nervously, as if she was the one who had been trapped in the Land Cruiser with Danish and his bodyguard.

'His father was a landowner from Tando Allahyar. I'm not sure how this was connected with anything but I'm guessing someone wanted to kidnap him.'

Khirad lowers her eyes and purses her lips into a thin line. I can tell that she too has a story to share but is not sure if she should disclose it. Her silence suddenly makes me want to shut up too, so I don't tell her more.

Danish, of course, is one of my tamer escapades. I almost got arrested a few years ago. But it wasn't my fault. My ex-boyfriend Aarij had parked his car (a Cultus, not a Land Cruiser) in a dark, secluded street near Seaview. It was close to New Year's Eve and security had been duly tightened. A cop saw us locked in each other's arms and threatened to take us to the *thana*.

Aarij tried to bribe him with 1,000 rupees and got thrashed for having the audacity to offer such a small sum. That's when I pulled out a press card from my purse.

'Tanya,' Khirad says as she pays the Careem chauffeur. 'This one's on me.'

'Don't be silly, Khirad.'

'Chill, I owe you one,' she says as she winks at me. 'After all, I'm the one who snatched your byline for the day.'

We grab a seat at the dhaba and Khirad glances through the menu. As I scan the crowd for a *nain nazara* – I refuse to use the term 'eye candy' for the men I fancy, especially after observing Hassan and his *taaru* ways – I spot my old friend Adam and wave at him. He's not one of the men I'd check out, escaping this honour on a technicality – he came out of the closet a few years ago.

Anyway, I'm glad I had the good sense to wear something nice – skin-tight jeans always go well with a white T-shirt and a brown scarf. At least I look better than that dowdy-looking woman he's sitting with. I bet she's one of his friends from art school – the type who always look like they've spent days in a sauna of cigarette smoke.

Adam notices me, waves and walks over to our table.

'Hey Tanya,' Adam says. 'What are you doing here?'

'I should be asking you this question. Didn't you have a date today?'

'Oh him.' His face contorts in disappointment. 'Yeah it went well. Poor boy had to go to a *marsiya* later so it was rather brief. He invited me to it though. I guess that's how Shia boys tell you they like you.'

I let out a hoarse laugh. Khirad stares impassively at Adam, wondering how she should react.

'Oh, where are my manners,' I say, knowing perfectly well that I have none. 'Adam, meet my ... friend ... Khirad. She's an education reporter at the *Daily Image*. Khirad, this is Adam. He's one of the most talented young artists in the city.'

'*The* most talented,' Adam corrects me.

'Hi, Adam. Nice to meet you,' Khirad says, stuttering as the words stream out of her mouth.

'It's nice to meet you too.'

By now, Adam's companion has turned around, looked at Adam and checked her wristwatch a couple of times.

'You better run along, Adam,' I say, holding a cigarette between my fingers and lighting it. 'Your little lady friend is getting jealous.'

'*Yaar*, screw her.' He yawns and stretches his hands above his shoulders. 'The girl needed some "artistic" inspiration. When I need that, I go find myself a man.'

'Maybe she's doing the same. Go give it to her and we'll talk later.'

Adam clenches his fists and points two middle fingers at me.

'Love ya,' I say, waving at him as he walks back to his table.

'So ... umm ... he's a gay?' Khirad asks me when Adam is out of earshot.

'Umm, it's just gay, sweetie. "A gay" makes him sound like an object. Not the animal that he is.'

'My mistake,' she replies quickly. 'I meant no offence. I've just never met a gay man before.'

Her response comes as a surprise to me. I expected her to be homophobic in addition to being a desperate husband-snatcher – it goes without saying doesn't it?

'Anyway, I'm just glad we're out of that event,' Khirad exhales. 'Let's order.'

She orders two kahwas and a pizza paratha for herself. I think she doesn't care too much about what the *rishta* aunties will say. Why should she? Even in the best case scenario, they won't be able to find her someone as eligible as Hassan.

It must be easy being Khirad, with her overbearing patron who takes her on exotic holidays. Who cares if her stories are riddled with syntactic errors and spelling mistakes? A lonely, undersexed subeditor can fix everything for her and no one will ever know any better. Meanwhile, I'm dreaming about Pukhtun men at hotels in Bannu and making a living out of correcting commas. But I guess I'm not entirely the subeditor stereotype since I'm definitely not undersexed.

'So you're not going to get yourself a Nutella paratha?' Khirad breaks into my thoughts.

'*Ugh*, why did you have to bring them up! I was just beginning to forget about them.'

But wait, why am I denying myself? Am I giving in to Mummy's insecurities?

'Don't be silly. Why should you be concerned about your figure? You look gorgeous. Any man would be thrilled to have you,' Khirad says firmly.

How do I tell this woman that men have already had me – or, should I say, I've had them? But that's not the point.

'It's not about men having me, Khirad,' I say, as the waiter brings my kahwa in a glass mug and places it on the table. 'I call the shots here. Not some mama's boy who occasionally thinks with his dick so that he can save brain cells.'

Khirad gulps down her drink and I mentally scold myself for being crude again. She's clearly not used to it.

'So, is there someone in your life?' she asks.

'Well, not at the moment.' I bow my head to stop a fly from landing on my nose. 'At least not someone who has stuck around. What about you?'

I take a swig of my kehwa and watch as her smile disappears.

'Well, since we're sharing ... it's ... well ... who you think it is.'

I'm outraged. How can Khirad think I care enough to know about her romantic escapades? Am I that transparent?

'Hassan?' I say, trying to sound nonchalant and slightly bored.

'Well ... since the cat is out of the bag,' she murmurs, perhaps throwing in an idiom to really drive the truth home. 'It is him.'

Well, well, well. I deserve a pat on my back for sniffing this secret out. Come to think of it, I might have been the first one to spread the rumour about Hassan and Khirad's affair. Now that Khirad has admitted it, I suppose I've been exonerated.

'Khirad, you do know he's married?' I say, going for a concerned rather than judgemental tone.

'Yes,' she says with a conviction that stuns me. 'But he has promised to marry me.'

'And what about Bina?'

'She's on her way out.'

'Oh, please,' I scoff involuntarily as I balance the glass mug on my knee. 'I've been hearing that for years. She's not going anywhere. I'm sure more girls like yourself will flit in and out before she decides to go.'

Khirad listens quietly. I know I'm being cruel, but my words seem to have pushed her into the realm of a reality that she has conveniently avoided all these months. I tell you, I should do this for a living. Who needs a shrink when they can have me? All I would need to do is feign interest in people's boring lives and offer brazen reality checks at a premium price. But business prospects aside, Khirad is in a wretched state. I never thought I would, but I feel sorry for this desi Anna Karenina as she pensively sips her kahwa and blinks back tears. I think I should say something – anything – to make her feel better.

'You know, I've also slept with another woman's man,' I say, startled by my own honesty. I could have casually changed the conversation to politics or the weather. But no, I have to get all personal diary about this. What happened to all those reservations I've harboured about Khirad? Did we declare some sort of a stalemate because of our shared dislike of Alan Trump or the *rishta* aunties? I don't know. There's just too much going on today. My mind needs time, sleep and a cigarette to recover from the confusion.

'Who was he?' Khirad whispers, her inquiring eyes demanding a secret in exchange for what she has told me.

Ignoring her question, I scavenge through my bag for my cell phone and call Hafeez.

'Hi T, I was just going to call you...'

'Oh,' I interrupt him. 'Do you want advice on what tie to wear for the wedding tonight? Don't opt for the lime green one you wore to Saleha's mehndi. It's a bit tacky and ... well ... in bad taste.'

'Tanya, there is going to be no wedding. Saad eloped with Mopsy.'

Notes on a Sandal

7 September 2016

7 p.m.

'I think I need to leave,' I tell Khirad, still staring at my phone. 'Sonia's fiancé has left her.'

'Oh no! That's devastating,' she says, fidgeting with the bracelet on her almost nervously, as if she and not Mopsy has snatched Saad from Sonia.

'You should go comfort her,' she continues, struggling to make eye contact with me. 'I'll make a move as well. It's a long way from here to Jamshed Road.'

Khirad hugs me, then takes a rickshaw home. I realize that something about Sonia's broken engagement has upset her. I should meet her at some point next week and ask her how she's doing. Why not? After all, charity begins at work for journalists, since none of us ever have the time to go home.

7.25 p.m.

I get into a Careem after a long telephone battle with an errant driver who couldn't follow my instructions properly. As I shut the door behind me, I notice that the Captain – a young man in jeans and a red T-shirt – is watching me from his rearview mirror to gauge my mood.

'If only you'd arrived on time, you wouldn't have to fear me so much,' I say, anger boiling inside me and finding release in a deep voice that I cannot recognize as my own.

'Sorry, madam,' he responds as he reverses his Cultus on to the main road. 'There was no water at my house in Landhi. So I stopped the car and was trying to find a solution.'

'How would you stopping the car in the middle of the road have made any difference?'

'Madam, my son was doing number two in the washroom,' he says hesitatingly, unsure if he should be sharing his son's poop schedule with me. 'My wife didn't know what to do. So she called me.'

He falls silent, as if expecting a reaction from me. I press my hands against my mouth to suppress the urge to chuckle but cannot control myself. The Captain throws a sideward glance at me as I recover from a laughing fit over the sheer absurdity of his explanation.

'*Waise*, I can help you find a solution to your water problem,' I say, still giggling at his candid response..

'What, madam?' he looks quizzically at me through the rearview mirror. 'My friend, whose house you're dropping me to, can cry you a river,' I say, a sliver of remorse creeping into my heart as I utter these words and poke fun at Sonia's misery. 'That one can fill your tanks with her tears whenever she's upset.'

The Captain laughs, accidentally breaks a traffic signal, narrowly averts a collision with a wailing bus and cusses under his breath.

'I'm not kidding when I say this,' I say, a bit surprised by how easily my anger towards him has been replaced with easy camaraderie. 'The city's water woes would be resolved if my friend got jilted on a daily basis.'

'Then, madam, we should make her the prime minister,' he says, honking at a motorcyclist who is attempting to overtake the car.

'Obviously, who else will become the next PM? Imran? I doubt it.'

'*Sahi bola*, madam,' he says, exhilarated by this political turn our conversation seems to have taken. 'People can sniff out a *budboo* easily these days.

'But I doubt Imran will bring his *tabdeeli*,' my driver waves a hand in the air and then places it on the gear stick. 'If Altaf Bhai couldn't keep his party together, how can an ageing cricketer keep his team intact? This isn't cricket. It's politics.'

I sigh but remain quiet. It's not because I disagree with him but because I need to prepare myself to meet Sonia. My Careem Captain understands my desire for silence. He stops spewing venom against Imran and focuses on the road.

As we turn on to 26th Street, concerns about Sonia's mysterious string of bad luck surfaces in my mind. Although I partly blame myself for my friend's misfortune, Hafeez labours under the illusion that it has something to do with that uncle of hers whose name was mentioned during the Panama leaks for owning offshore accounts.

'These things can have an impact on you,' he had told me seriously.

As the car swerves onto Khayaban-e-Shaheen, a numbing fear settles into my heart and my legs go weak with worry. Memories of our unforgotten college years return to me, reminding me how difficult it is to handle a teary-eyed, depressed Sonia.

8 p.m.

I find myself outside Sonia's house and am about to press the bell when my phone begins to ring. Thankfully, it's Topsy and not Hafeez with more bad news about Sonia.

'Did you hear the good news?' Topsy's voice rings through the phone. 'You know, about my sister whisking your friend's fiancé away.'

'Topsy, this is no laughing matter,' I say grimly, rising to Sonia's defence. 'Poor Sonia must be devastated.'

'I'm sure. But she ought to be used to it. After all, you did the same thing to her,' Topsy says. 'That girl is clearly no lightweight. She's experienced more heartbreak than Devdas.'

'What does that even mean? Devdas only loved once.'

'So did Sonia. *Bechari*, double-crossed in love. Too bad she's a doormat. I'd feel sorry for her otherwise.'

'Don't be cruel. She's vulnerable as fuck.'

'Actually, she's stupid as fuck. Sonia chooses to surround herself with all the wrong people. No wonder she's devastated. Her friend got to shag her fiancé before she could. And now he's run off before she could pin him down.'

A uniformed security guard unlocks the gate and smiles when he recognizes me. I walk towards Sonia's house.

'Is there a point to this conversation? You know, apart from calling me out for being a homewrecker.'

'Oh don't be silly,' Topsy lets out a squeak of outrage. 'Mopsy's the one who's the homewrecker. You're the drunken mistake, the one-night stand. Honestly, who better than me knows about losing a husband? Yes, it sucks, but that doesn't mean that you should forget how Sonia believed Saad and didn't even ask for your version of the story. Don't feel sorry for her just because she's been jilted.'

It's a rare moment when Topsy reflects on her failed marriage. She's always hidden her pain from me, even when I've tried to pry with endless onslaughts of questions. For a long time, I was her impressionable younger friend whose innocence she found solace in. She seems to be opening up now, but it's bad timing, unfortunately.

'But, listen, let's talk later. I'm at the doormat's door.'

'Sounds painful. I don't get why you still try with her.'

'Topsy, we've been over this before,' I say, unable to disguise my irritation. 'Sonia said sorry and we made up.'

'Right, she totally meant it and you totally forgave her. Anyway, now that you're there, remember to give her a message.'

'From you? I'm not here to add insult to injury.'

'Screw that. Just tell the doormat to hang in there. Things could be worse. Also, tell her Mopsy says hi.'

Topsy guffaws happily as she hangs up. I am feeling irritated with her, but she might have a point. Why the hell am I here? What will this visit achieve? I just hope Sonia doesn't bring up the one-night stand. I don't want to be rude to her at a time like this. It would only distract people from Sonia's misery and I'd be accused of stealing the spotlight.

8.05 p.m.

'My sandal,' Sonia shouts as I walk into her room. 'Where's my red sandal? Chhoti Apa, *kidhar gayi meri* sandal?'

'Chill out, Sonia,' Hafeez says lazily, notices me and flashes me an amused smile. 'You'll find it.'

'But ... but ... I was going to wear it tonight.'

'Sonia, please...' Hafeez says. 'Look, Tanya's here too. She'll help you look for it.'

'Tanya!' Sonia squeals. Her face is puffy with crying, and there are dark streaks on her face, cutting across the layers of rouge on her cheeks. 'Oh my god, Saad. He just ... he just ... you warned me ... and I didn't listen.'

'I'm so sorry, *jaan*,' I say, unsure of how to placate her. 'But ... err ... Allah *aur dega*, you know.'

Hafeez's eyes widen and he presses his hand against his mouth to contain his giggles. He looks ridiculous, like a schoolboy who is still learning how to be discreet. Sonia ignores the snide remark and continues to look for her red sandals.

'Saad bought them for me!' she exclaims. 'I was going to wear them for our wedding night.'

Sonia's delusional outburst doesn't shock me as much as her fiancé's strange demand. Of all the things Saad could tell his wife to wear on their wedding night! Footwear? Is this some new fetish? Did Saad elope with the wrong sister?

'I was going to wear it for our first...' Sonia pauses, as if her train of thought has been disrupted by an epiphany. 'Wait just a bloody second, you slept with Saad too. You, you, you ... lousy bitch!'

'Sonia, calm down,' Hafeez steps in as Sonia moves towards me.

'Why should I? It's not my fault he left me. It's people like Tanya and Mopsy who took him away from me.'

'I think I should go, Hafeez,' I say, turning towards the door.

'Get out!' Sonia flings a black sandal at me. It misses by an inch. 'You man-stealing bitch! Like father, like daughter. Don't fucking come back!'

Tears sting my eyes at this humiliation but I refuse to cry. As I stumble down the stairs, I run into Sonia's maid, Chhoti Apa. I've known her since Sonia and I became friends in college. We had made a futile attempt to teach her English back then.

'How are you, Tanya *beti*?' Chhoti Apa asks. She's holding a shoebox in her hands.

'I'm fine, Chhoti Apa,' I say as I hug her.

'Very bad news, all this,' she shakes her head in distress and her hand travels to her forehead.

'*Ji*, it's sad.' After being thrown out of Sonia's room so unceremoniously, I do not have the will or the energy to sympathize with Chhoti Apa's ward.

'*Bas beti, jo uske naseeb main hai,*' Chhoti Apa says and looks heavenwards.

I take that as a cue and dash towards the gate. It's been a feverishly long day. I've gone from making a friend in Khirad to losing one in Sonia, but really, what had I expected would happen? Maybe Bakhtu Bhai should have just bludgeoned me with an axe when he had the chance.

11 p.m.

After taking a long shower and gorging on a plate of leftover biryani, I sit in my room and browse through my phone, hoping to forget the day's misadventures. There are four missed calls from Hafeez, but I'm not in the mood to put more strain on my restless mind and go over what Sonia did.

My phone buzzes softly. This time, it's a text from Hafeez.

'Hope you aren't upset,' he says. Just a single sentence, but I can sense that he's worried about me. A second text follows immediately after. 'Give Sonia some time. She'll come around. It's just that the whole thing is even worse because Saad called off the engagement by having his mother call Sonia's mother. He hasn't even spoken to Sonia directly.'

Anger and a seething hatred for Saad crawls into my heart as I read the message.

'The least Sonia deserved was a dignified break-up.' I punch out a response to Hafeez's message. 'This is downright insensitive. A dick move from a man who barely has one.'

Once the message is sent, I think about the first time I met Sonia – the day the admissions list came out at SZABIST. When I entered the university to check the admissions list, there had been a crowd in front of the bulletin board – students muttering frantic prayers and checking for their names. Unwilling to surrender to common hysteria, I had busied myself by looking into a mirror that hung in the lobby. Sonia, who also has a narcissistic streak, was doing the same thing. Our eyes met and we had smiled at each other – instantly connected and in sync. We've been friends since.

I can't let such an old friendship go. I need to speak to Saad and convince him to talk to Sonia. Everyone deserves closure, even if they fling sandals at friends and insist on judging people based to what their parents did.

11.10 p.m.

'How'd it go, babe?' Topsy asks with characteristic indifference, as soon as I pick up her call. 'Did the doormat cry like a baby? Does she miss my new brother-in-law?'

'Sonia threw a sandal at me,' I say, still wincing at the memory. 'She's never gotten violent with me. I guess she's standing up for herself.'

'Good for her,' disinterest creeps into Topsy's voice. 'Oh well, Saad and Mopsy's wedding reception is on *chand raat*. You better come. It's on the twelfth at a chalet at DHA Golf Club. It's a small affair and we're not inviting many people.'

'Wait, I can't do that,' I say. My heart gallops at the mere suggestion of attending Saad's wedding. 'He just dumped Sonia. My friends will hate me if I go. Hafeez will be super pissed. Also, have you completely forgotten about my little incident with Saad?'

'Honey, you're the only one who still remembers it,' her words prick me with their scathing honesty. 'Anyway, the doormat chucked you out. And I don't understand why you insist on taking what that office boy says so seriously. Does he matter so much to you?'

'Hafeez? Oh, he matters.'

Topsy giggles, amused by my earnestness. She gets a high from exploring even the vaguest possibility of potential love in any relationship. But all I feel for Hafeez is friendship. That's all. He does wear his pants well, I won't deny that. And off late, I might have started caring a bit more than I thought I did. But there's no way I'm telling Topsy that.

'Screw them, come as my friend,' Topsy says, sensing my reservations and changing the subject. 'You don't need to hang around the newly-weds. And there's going to be free booze.'

Topsy still harbours the illusion that I'm friends with her for the free booze. She doesn't realize that I've evolved since the early days of our friendship. Back then I was dependent on her for all the goodies that entice the young and the reckless. Now I'm just friends with her for the expensive booze when I can't afford it on an empty bank balance. I stopped smoking hash when Mummy confused its smell with my natural body odour and insisted on buying me deodorant. But I can always trust Hafeez or my bootlegger to get me the local *maal*.

'I do miss drinking champagne and schmoozing with the rich, famous and downright dirty,' I tell Topsy, weighing my options.

Good booze aside, I can also use this opportunity to talk to Saad. Of course, I can't let Topsy know I'm doing that. No one needs to know. I'm not trying to win a popularity contest. I'm just trying to be a good friend.

'Keep it hushed, okay?' I tell Topsy. 'I'll see you then.'

After she hangs up, I lie in bed and ponder over the heady experiences I've been through today – Sonia's lost sandal and virulent temper, Khirad's confession about the affair between her and Hassan, Topsy and Saad's elopement. I jab a thumb and finger across my forehead to ease my migraine. As sleep laps over me in its benevolence, I wonder if I did the right thing by accepting Topsy's invitation. Will Sonia catch me at the party and throw another shoe at me?

Desi Chinese and the Danger Zone

12 September 2016

9.40 a.m.

I roll out of bed to the clamour of yet another domestic spat. Mummy, Lurch and Adila the cleaning lady are shouting at each other, and their defeaning shrieks and cries are all too familiar now. Who needs an alarm clock when you can wake up to a raging family drama?

I wobble down the stairs to be a spectator to the latest conflict.

'*Baji, Allah ki kasam,*' Adila pinches and pulls at the supple skin on her neck. 'I cleaned the bathroom yesterday. He's a liar. Ask him when he cleaned the kitchen last?'

'*Chup kar*, Adila,' Lurch bellows. He raises a clenched hand in the air, as if to strike her.

'*Ek* second,' Mummy says. She waves her manicured nails at them, turns to me and pinches the bridge of her nose. 'I'm getting sick of these people. Tanya, you deal with them for a change. Your *bechari* ma has grown too old for their shenanigans.'

'Why do you have to drag me into all this, Mummy?' I stretch my hands behind my shoulders and walk back towards the stairs. 'I have work to do. My school textbooks story is going into print tomorrow and I need to go visit a government school nearby. Do you know how difficult it was to find a school that was open a day before Eid? I can't be wasting time meddling in their affairs.'

'Why?' Mummy roars, outraged by my indifference. 'Is this not your house? Or is your father's house your only home?'

'*Tauba*, Mummy!' I shout as I walk back to my room. 'Why would you say such a thing? Why would I care about a house I've never even been to?'

Okay. That isn't entirely true. As I enter my room, I guiltily recall the time I'd gone over to Step-Mummy's house under false pretenses. I was younger then and cared about my parents' marriage. I kept it a secret from Mummy because I knew that she'd taunt me about it for the rest of her life and mine. For my mother, a five-timer with a reserved seat in heaven, such transgressions could only mean one thing – Step-Mummy was doing *kaala jaadu* on me.

Driven by a desire for complete secrecy, I had considered the possibility of visiting Step-Mummy's house as a census worker. That way, I'd have a legitimate reason to enquire about how many children Daddy and Step-Mummy had.

So I decided to take Sonia along for my sleuthing expedition. This was before the Saad affair and we were inseparable, our intimacy unmarked by rifts and petty rivalries.

'Remember,' I had told her after I'd parked the car outside Seaview Apartments and inhaled the tangy sea breeze. 'Don't mention anything about Daddy. My name isn't Tanya. It's Tehzeeb. Okay?'

'*Uff*,' Sonia had cooed. 'What a name! Can I be Umrao?'

'Sure, if you're masquerading as an old-school hooker.'

My first meeting with my stepmother was quite shocking, if not altogether anticlimactic. When I look back at it now, I still find it difficult to understand how Daddy could leave a woman like Mummy – who never misses a botox appointment – for that woman. If Mummy – at her designer best – is a model in a L'oreal commercial, Step-Mummy is the 'before' section of the ad. Maybe Daddy was feeling nostalgic and missed Mummy's youthful gawkiness.

'I'm Tehzeeb,' I told Step-Mummy when she opened the door to her apartment. 'This is ...'

'Umrao ... Umrao Ada,' my partner-in-crime said, holding out her hand as if she were an heiress with no finesse. Step-Mummy didn't shake her hand.

'We're here to meet Tabassum,' I said, trying to put on a *pendu* accent so that my true identity was not disclosed. 'You know, my friend Tabs.'

Step-Mummy was left speechless. I couldn't blame her. Words could not describe how transparent our lies were. I half-expected her to endearingly pat me on the cheek and tell me how much my nose and eyes resemble Daddy's.

'Silly girl,' I imagined her saying, 'I know who you are. Go home to your mommy and leave your daddy with me.'

Her reaction wasn't as severe as I thought it would be. On the contrary, I found myself terrified when she opened her mouth and a string of disconnected words tumbled out.

'Sorry, girls,' Step-Mummy replied. 'Tabassum no live here. You get wrong house. Me live here with my half.'

Unimpressed by the woman who had whisked my father away from me, I left the apartment. The only bright spot in that evening was Sonia's awful impersonation of Umrao Jaan – she truly has a knack for being absurd.

Anyway, Mummy and Daddy never officially got divorced. He still comes around to check up on us. We've become indifferent to his presence. For any visitor to our house, my father's absence is like a large elephant in an otherwise empty room. I think Hassan was the one who, rather rudely, used that idiom to describe our 'situation' when he and Bina visited us a few months ago. Fortunately for us, Mummy handles the situation in her own eccentric way. No one in our house misses the old elephant anymore. Unless Mummy has been keeping her longings secret all these years in the faint hope that Daddy will return to her.

10.45 a.m.

I enter a small, decrepit classroom at Maryland Government School near Zamzama. Mrs Khalida

Masood, the school's principal, whispers into the class teacher's ear. The teacher smiles politely but coldly at me, as if she secretly wishes to see my obituary in tomorrow's newspaper for disrupting her class.

'Sorry about putting you through the trouble, Khalida-*ji*.' I hold her wrist. 'I just thought I'd speak to the children myself and ask them what they know about Pakistan's history. I want the story to assess learning outcomes.'

She throws a suspicious frown at me.

'It's all right,' Khalida says, tapping the teacher's wrist in a conciliatory gesture. 'She won't mind.'

The class teacher lifts her brow and walks over to the blackboard. 'Ask away, Ms Shaukat. The children will answer. Won't you?'

The children watch me in silence, appraising my movements like a predator would its prey.

'What do you know about Jinnah?' I ask a boy seated in the front row. As he rises from his seat, his face reddens. He opens his mouth to say something but breaks into laughter. He lowers his eyes in shame as the principal frowns at him.

'Answer Miss, Sajid,' her irritable voice resonates through the classroom then dips into a soft murmur. 'Tell Ms Shaukat. Who is Jinnah?'

'He is the founder of Pakistan,' the boy responds coyly. 'The best Muslim.'

The students clap loudly, confident that Sajid's answer is the truth and nothing but the truth.

'And who was in the subcontinent before Muhammad bin Qasim came to Sindh?' My second question subdues the thunderous roar of clapping and the classroom is filled with a breathless silence. The students look at each other, pull out their textbooks and flip through the pages to search for a plausible answer to my question.

'Ms Shaukat,' the teacher's voice rises. '*I assure you*, I've taught these children well.'

I watch the teacher resume her lesson. As the principal and I leave the classroom, I shudder at the thought that the future of the nation rests securely in her hands.

11.45 a.m.

I return home, park myself in the living room and type out the story that will get me the byline I've been craving all week. My phone rings as I type the first sentence.

'How was Maryland?' Khirad's voice penetrates through the receiver.

'I've spent the last four days visiting government schools to assess biases in the way history has been taught,' I say, exhaling audibly to release a hundred years of exhaustion. 'I'm sick of getting sneered at by teachers who think I'm trying to prove to the world that they aren't doing their jobs right.'

'You're the one who insisted on visiting classrooms,' Khirad says. 'I always get such information from annual reports.'

'Yeah, but I wanted to see it for myself.' I return to hammering on the keyboard. 'You know how your Hassan is. He never lets me do the stories I want to do. When he does, he always finds faults in them and insists that I should stick to the T2F events that he expects me to cover. This time around, he's been indulgent only because you've been helping me with contacts.'

'Don't be silly, he values what you do,' Khirad says, rising to her paramour's defence. 'He told everyone at the office that your story will be printed in the Eid edition of the paper.'

'Sure, that does wonders for my career as a journalist,' I respond sardonically. 'No hard-working adult reads the papers on Eid.'

'Don't worry,' Khirad consoles me. 'I'm sure it'll be the best story this Eid.'

12 noon

A phone call from an official from the education department distracts me as I write the final paragraph. I had spoken to him yesterday regarding my story. Much to my disappointment, he wants to retract his statement.

'Madam, this is a controversial story,' the official tells me. '*Bara masla ho jayega*. My boss will kill me for talking to the press.'

'But surely you realize that your name isn't going in the story?' I say, hoping against hope that he'll change his mind.

'Yes, but madam, he will know it is me.'

I am seriously annoyed, and for a moment, I wonder whether I should leave his comment in the story just to spite him. But the poor guy deserves a chance at life. Why kill him with my pen when I could target someone more deserving?

With profound sadness, I press the delete button. The official's comment disappears, taking with it all the startling insights I had gleaned about how content is decided for history textbooks taught at government schools. As my story shrinks to half its original size, my heart sinks in despair. I'm tempted to delete the entire story, crawl under the sheets and hide. But the smouldering desire to prove Hassan wrong and to complete the unfinished paragraph tugs me out of my misery. I take a deep breath and return to my piece with renewed gusto.

12.30 p.m.

My phone beeps minutes after I submit my story. I've already jumped into bed for a quick nap. I lazily crawl out of bed and stumble towards the dressing table where I've left my phone to charge.

I open my inbox and see a message from Hafeez. I click open the message and read it with a strange relish.

'Remember, the deadline for the pages is earlier today because of chand raat. Let's try to be out of there by 8.'

Hafeez seems to be quite eager about the Eid holidays. He plans to wrap up early, even though there are forces beyond our control – like the moon playing hide-and-seek – that will determine whether tomorrow will be Eid or not.

I reply – 'I'll be in by two. Just promise me that the stories will be filed earlier. I have to be somewhere.'

His response comes in a few minutes later. 'Ah, sounds like you're living it up on chand raat. Can I assume I'm invited?'

I reply – 'You're mighty cocky, aren't you? But no, you aren't invited. Too bad.'

Hafeez ignores my jibe. His next text comes in. 'Hurry on over. We can grab lunch in the cafeteria. Maqsood Bhai has desi Chinese food today.'

I will never understand Hafeez's fascination for desi Chinese food. His obsession has surpassed all limits of sanity and good judgement.

I thumb a reply to Hafeez's message. 'Fine, I'll try to be at work sooner than usual.'

A lot has changed between Hafeez and I since the night Sonia flung a sandal at me and I accepted Topsy's invitation to Saad's wedding. Encumbered by guilt and the fear of Hafeez's harsh scrutiny, I've established a quiet emotional distance from him over the last few days. But even though his clumsiness tends to cripple him in social situations, he can sharply detect any changes in our friendship. Throughout the week, he's asked me if everything is all right. I've kept quiet because I know that if I say anything, I'll spill out unwanted details and hurt people in irreversible ways.

1 p.m.

'Tanya, come eat with me today.' Mummy stops me at the door as I prepare to leave for work.

Every Monday, Mummy is in a quiet frenzy because she's famished. She tells Lurch to prepare dal and slurps it with a spoon like its soup. This is part of the self-denial mode she slips into at the beginning of every week.

'Mummy, I need to run.'

'Fine, run away,' she bellows. 'What am I anyway if not a burden? Load me into a truck and drop me off at Edhi Home.'

I'm tempted to be a good daughter for a change and do just as she says. But she'd drive everyone at Edhi Home insane. Poor Edhi Sahib would have tackled her with patience, may he rest in peace. But I am doubtful about the rest of the inmates.

'Chill, Mummy, why do you have to do so much drama?'

I sit down at the table next to her and watch her sip the dal with a dirty spoon.

'At least wash the spoon before you put it into your mouth.'

'I shouldn't,' she says, stirring the spoon in the bowl. 'Today I need to live like I'm beyond privilege and cannot even be touched by the demonic forces of pleasure.'

I roll my eyes. On my way to work, I should Google some mental asylums in the city as well. I could find one in Mauripur, add Mummy to its rolls and then pretend I can't visit her because the security situation in the city is abysmal. Then I would no longer have to watch her drink dal.

2 p.m.

'Don't worry about Sonia,' Hafeez tells me as he puts a spoonful of schezwan rice in his mouth. 'Give her some time to get over it. She'll be back at work after Eid. Everything will be fine.'

I turn to my cell phone and begin texting Topsy so I can avoid speaking about Sonia. My silence brings a scowl to Hafeez's face.

'Okay, this is getting out of hand,' he says as he drops the spoon on to his plate with a loud clatter. 'What's on your mind? Why are you suddenly so aloof? I know it has something to do with Sonia. You can't hide anything from me. Now spill.'

'Calm down,' I say, sending the message before I put my phone away. 'Nothing's wrong. I'm fine.'

'Is that right?' Hafeez raises his eyebrows. 'And what about this new friendship you've struck up with Khirad? Does that also come under your definition of "nothing's wrong"?'

'Hafeez, you sound like a broken record. Even Erdogan wasn't this insecure after the failed coup.'

'That reminds me,' Hafeez says, rising from his chair and forgetting the angry interrogation of just a moment ago. 'I must ask Khirad about her Pak-Turk school closure story. Or would you like to do the honour?'

I silently dial her number and wait for the line to connect.

'Hey, babe,' Khirad whispers when she picks up, her voice cracking. She's clearly upset, but I don't feel like getting involved.

'When are you filing the Pak-Turk story?'

'On its way, babe,' she says. 'It's just Hassan. He's being so difficult.'

What could have happened between them in a matter of hours? I should have realized that being friends with Khirad involves getting on an emotional roller-coaster that will pull me deeper into a vortex of drama and intrigue.

'What did he do now?'

I move away from the table where Hafeez and I are seated, as if the distance will help protect Khirad's secret from being disclosed.

'I told him to leave his wife,' she whispers over the phone. 'He's not willing to do that. And ...'

'And? What are you planning to do now?'

Khirad continues to whisper, as if she fears being heard.

'I've decided to call it quits,' she says, her voice choked with emotion.

Her reaction fills me with disappointment. I didn't expect her to relinquish her fight without a gun-blazing confrontation with Bina.

'Why give up so soon?' I hear myself say in cold defiance of the memories of Mummy's misery when Daddy left. 'What's the harm? You should march into his office and demand justice.'

She could also strut into Hassan's drawing room and challenge his wife to a duel. At least those with the good fortune of witnessing the brawl will have something to laugh about.

'I'm tired of fighting,' Khirad says. 'I just want peace.'

'Good for you,' I say, still hoping that she'll change her mind.

As I cut the call and return to the table, Hafeez's eyes bear questions that I cannot answer.

'Is all well?' he asks, spooning the remnants of his Chinese food into his mouth.

'Yes, all is well.' I lower my head and fidget with my fingers.

'Where is the Pak-Turk story?' Hafeez asks, his eyes transfixed on mine.

'The story is … on its way,' I stammer, turning away from him.

'You seemed to be talking about something top-secret,' he says as he gulps down some water. 'Does she have a huge stack of black money stashed away on a sunny island in Panama?'.

I ignore Hafeez's question. His crestfallen face fills me with fear – a peculiar discontent that I cannot comprehend.

'You should tell your friend that not every secret is sacred,' Hafeez says. Then he grins and walks out of the cafeteria.

4 p.m.

'All set for tonight's party?'

Relief washes over me as I hear Topsy's voice over the phone. It pulls me out of the dark thoughts I was having because of a shoddily written report about a robbery in Liaquatabad. The robbery had been planned by the house owner's second wife' and the details were more morbid than I had expected them to be.

'Yeah,' I absentmindedly tell Topsy. 'Though I'm scared I'll get into trouble for going to Mopsy's wedding reception.'

'Don't be silly. What are you scared of? That Sonia? Besides, I must introduce you to my Lahori boy. His friend will be coming as well. He's a journalist too. I think you'll hit it off.'

'Why? Because we're both obsessed with the news and will have shared orgasms over India's statements about Gilgit-Baltistan and Balochistan?'

'India's what?' Topsy sounds clueless. 'I just thought you'd get along because neither of you can resist a dry martini and vodka.'

'Oh, look at you, using alcohol as a litmus test to make matches. Isn't that smart? Why expect match-making to happen in heaven when you can bring people together on earth with a couple of tequila shots?'

'You have no idea how important it can be, love. Okay, don't be late. Our guest will be waiting for you.'

Topsy hurriedly hangs up and I return to editing the story. As I type the lede sentence, I wonder if the Lahori hunk's friend will be just like him. My trepidation grows as I contemplate the dangerous possibility of him flogging me in the bedroom. There are some fetishes that are best left unexplored.

5 p.m.

Sonia has filed a story about some hospital employees who were unfairly sacked for protesting against their delayed promotions. As the story lands in my inbox, I am impressed by Sonia's ability to bounce back.

'I told her to file a story,' Hafeez tells me. 'I thought it would be good for her to get back to work. Also, *you* should edit the story. It'll be good for your friendship.'

'Your bright ideas just keep pouring in, don't they now?' I say with mild sarcasm.

He laughs and beams a smile at me. 'Let's keep the channels of communication open.'

I look away, a little embarrassed at my own reluctance to salvage my relationship with Sonia.

'Tanya…' Hafeez's voice rings through the hum of the ceiling fan. I turn to face him. He continues to peer into his computer screen.

'What?' I blurt out instinctively.

'You're doing it again,' he replies, his eyes fixed on his screen and his fingers hammering away on the keyboard. 'You're being evasive.'

'*Ugh* ... you're still a broken record,' I say, knowing perfectly well how irascible I sound to Hafeez. 'Screw that, I'm just going into zen mode now so I can edit that bloody story.'

Hafeez continues to stare at his screen. The rattle of his keyboard subsides. I quickly click open the email containing Sonia's story. Moments later, all I can hear is the sound of my fingers pressing against the keyboard. Hafeez has walked out of the room with his cigarette and lighter.

5.15 p.m.

Much to my dismay, Sonia's story leaves me full of questions and an unexplained fury. She seems to have bounced back from her misery but without any professional integrity.

'Hafeez, she hasn't included the hospital's version,' I say, aware that I sound even more irritated than I usually do. 'Why is she trying to get us into trouble? Does she not realize that she needs to give us a complete story?'

'Easy, just call and ask her for one,' Hafeez says, turning towards me.

His reply doesn't reassure me. I continue to seethe with anger.

'But I can say one thing with certainty,' I mutter to myself. 'It is obvious that Sonia didn't get this story from a Careem chauffeur.'

I'm not being snarky when I say this. Each time Sonia manages to pluck out facts from a Captain, the choice, stamina and intensity of her words is quite different. There is a semblance of truth to what she is saying and her train of thought follows logic.

'Don't say that,' Hafeez says. 'She's trying her best.'

I scoff at his explanation and turn to my phone.

5.20 p.m.

As I stare at the computer screen, I hum the lyrics to Billie Holiday's *'Don't explain'* in my head and keep time with my feet. I'm delaying having a conversation with Sonia. After a few minutes, I rise from my seat, stretch my arms in the air and yawn, undaunted by the presence of colleagues who, I know, will silently judge me for acting unladylike.

I walk out into the smoking area for a quick cigarette break and check out the new guy in office, who is puffing away on an otherwise vacant bench in the smoking area.

When I return from my break, I tweak the edited copy of Sonia's incomplete story. After a second read, the story truly does seem like an amateurish attempt instead of professional journalism. The sentences are raw, reflective and, at times, written in poor taste. The dangling modifiers, the spelling errors and, *uff,* the misplaced punctuation will make it all the more difficult to fix this piece.

I change the word 'sacking' to 'dismissal' because Sonia has used it more times in the story than she's been dumped over the years. I move the final paragraph closer to the lede sentence because she just never knows how to end her stories. But my efforts do little to fix the piece or capture the essence of the story.

As I continue to buy time before I call Sonia, I wonder if this story is some form of revenge against me. She's capable of a lot worse than this. Sonia always knows when to strike and how to pull her punches.

5.30 p.m.

'Hi, Sonia. Tanya here,' I say, my voice unnaturally loud. 'I need a version from a hospital official on your employee dismissal story. Can you arrange that for me?'

I rush through everything in a single breath in case she decides to interrupt the flow of my thoughts with one of her wisecracks. At this point, Hafeez shifts closer to me and is eavesdropping on our conversation. I can't allow myself to get angry, otherwise he'll want to talk to me about it later.

'Umm. It's the day before Eid. There's no one at the hospital.'

She hangs up without allowing me the opportunity to respond. That's a relief. I thought she would relent midway and talk to me for hours about how she misses our friendship. That would have sabotaged my *chand raat* plans.

I guess there is a god. And he doesn't mind if I live a little, even if it is at another person's emotional expense.

'How'd it go?' Hafeez asks as I put down the receiver. 'Did you guys kiss and make up?'

'*Naaaa*, she was sweet about it. She just hung up.'

I grab a pack of cigarettes and go to the smoking area. Hafeez texts me later to ask how I'm holding up. His plans to get me to reconcile with Sonia are getting between me and my booze. But I still think he's got the best views this office has to offer. If only he wore better clothes.

I'm smoking when I get another message from him – 'It's Saad's wedding reception tonight. Sonia's just upset. Give her some time.'

Frankly, I'm the one who needs the time to distance myself from the situation. I should leave work earlier today and prepare for tonight.

6.30 p.m.

'He told me Bina is pregnant,' Khirad tells me in the smoking area as I take my umpteenth break for the day. 'He can't leave her.'

'They're having another child?' I ask. 'I never realized Hassan was so ... well ... alarmingly fertile. A man like him is better off impotent. Future generations might not forgive Bina for taking a dip in her husband's gene pool.'

Tears shimmer in Khirad's eyes, and I realize this might not be the best time to rag on Hassan.

'Screw him, you shouldn't have even an iota of sympathy for such a man,' I say, hoping I sound genuinely supportive.

'I wish there was a way to get back at him,' Khirad says as she wipes her tears and stares pensively at her phone screen.

'Send him a packet of condoms and put an end to this whole charade,' I say, recklessly.

Khirad looks up from her phone and eyes me with consternation.

'And what will that achieve?'

'Well, uh,' I stammer, still unsure as to why I'd suggest something like that. 'It'll be a lot of fun. Plus, it'll drive home the point.'

I walk out of the smoking area, hoping that she'll forget my suggestion. But she sniggers as she follows me out.

'His reaction to finding a packet of Durex in the mail would be priceless,' she laughs.

'I wonder what Bina will think,' I laugh in return. 'Maybe she will assume that her husband doesn't want the child.'

'Don't worry,' Khirad whispers into my ear as she embraces me. 'That man doesn't deserve to be placed on a pedestal. I'll see to it that he's thrown off of it.'

I'm beginning to question Khirad's raw simplicity. Hassan has clearly rattled the wrong woman. He should fear the wrath of her vengeance.

7.30 p.m.

'I'm off, Hafeez.' I collect my bag from my desk. 'The pages are all set to be transferred ahead and the moon has finally revealed herself to the maulvis who've been checking her out all evening. Tomorrow is Eid.'

Hafeez rises from his seat. His gaze meets mine. I look away and rummage through my bag with feigned urgency. I feel like a schoolgirl who has been caught for an ill-disguised prank or lie. Does Hafeez have an inkling about where I'm going tonight?

'Yeah, but I thought you'd stay for a bit. I thought we could hang out and I could drop you home later.'

'Not tonight, Hafeez. Mummy wants help with household chores and I have plans for the night.'

'Really? And you agreed to the chores without even staging a protest? I'm disappointed.'

'Yeah, true.' Oh god, all my lies are so transparent – like that see-through dress I once ordered online which nearly sent Mummy to the emergency room. I should make a quick exit before he floods me with further questions and identifies the deception behind my monosyllabic responses.

I pull my phone out of my bag and pretend to read a text message.

'Oh damn, Mummy wants to begin ASAP. I have to run. Bye.'

'*Ah-han* ... bye ... Eid Mubarak. Don't have too much fun.'

As I run towards the exit, I reflect on whether I've made a mistake by not confiding in Hafeez. Would he have understood my intentions or quashed them as a mere excuse for treachery? But I couldn't have taken the risk. His unwavering loyalty to Sonia would have clouded his judgement. I can't afford to lose his friendship over Sonia.

Murree, not Martini

Saad waves at me as I walk into the reception venue – a chalet at the Golf Club that flanks the Arabian Sea. I don't understand how he managed to spot me so quickly. The bungalow is teeming with bejewelled women clad in lehnga cholis and embellished ensembles. I guess Mummy was right though. My ice-blue chiffon shirt with pearl-sprayed bellbottoms does capture unwarranted attention.

I smile at him, hoping that he won't leave his dolled-up bride and come over to talk to me. Unfortunately, my hopes have a way of being crushed as soon I think them up.

'Hi, you,' Saad says as he jostles through the crowd to hug me. 'Haven't seen you in a while. How's my favourite leading lady?'

Marriage has sapped Saad's ability to flirt. The not-so-mighty under the sack have fallen in the mightiest of ways. 'Leading lady? Are you referring to Sonia?'

'Umm, no,' Saad lowers his head and fidgets with his hands.

'Do you expect me to make a secret excursion to the bedroom with you at your own wedding reception?' I ask contemptuously. I'm puzzled by my audacity. 'Save yourself the trouble, boyo. How about you drive over to Sonia's house and break up with her in a dignified manner? Why have someone else wipe your shit?'

'What can I say, Tanya?' his voice dips with regret. 'I should technically be apologizing to you since you're Sonia's friend. But then again, you're part of the reason why I realized I couldn't be with her. I wish I could repay you in some way.'

'Huh? Should I pat myself on the back for convincing you to call off your wedding?' I stare at him sternly, but I am forgetting how thick-skinned Saad is.

'You can do a lot more than just pat yourself on the back,' he smiles lecherously.

'Is that a trapped husband's plea, Saad? *Waise*, I didn't know I was the new antidote for marriage.'

'Your mum would be proud,' he sniggers.

If I told Mummy this, she'd be more than willing to shift to Edhi Home and behave herself just so she wouldn't have to see me again.

'How did I convince you not to marry Sonia?' I ask him, curious despite myself.

'Well, you helped me see what else was out there,' Saad says, taking a sip from a glass of red wine he's just lifted from a waiter. He moves his hand to my waist.

'Saad, tell me one thing.' I stare directly into his eyes as his lower lip touches the glass. 'Have you and Mopsy done it yet? Is she ... satisfied with you?'

He spits out his drink and coughs until he catches his breath. I purse my lips and stifle the rising urge to giggle.

'Easy there, don't panic,' I say. I untangle my arms from his shoulders. 'It was just a harmless question.'

Saad furrows his brows and give me the death stare. He doesn't reply but chugs down his wine and gags into his glass.

'Oh well,' I say, tapping my purse on his back as he begins to cough again. 'I think I see Topsy. I'll see you later.'

I walk away, leaving Saad to recover from his well-deserved near asphyxiation.

9.45 p.m.

'Tanya's a journalist,' Topsy distractedly tells Bilal as she hands me a snifter of martini. 'I told you about her, right?'

Bilal chuckles as he hugs me. He seems to have remembered an old joke or a sleazy thought.

'It's nice to finally meet you, Bilal,' I say. 'Topsy has told me so much about you. I'm glad there are a few good men left in the world these days.'

Bilal and Topsy look into each other's eyes and giggle conspiratorially.

'Well, we're quite an unconventional pair,' he says.

Ignoring the remark, I take a sip of my drink and wait for the lovebirds to stop laughing at their own joke.

'Where's Indrajeet?' Topsy asks Bilal as she recovers from her laughing fit. 'It's time to play matchmaker. Wait, I'll go find him.'

Topsy zips into a group of overdressed guests who gleefully swig cognac as they dance to loud music.

Minutes later, she is nowhere to be seen and Bilal and I are forced to schmooze with each other.

Clad in a white tee and a pair of dark jeans, Bilal looks nothing like the virile man I'd figured would be lying in Topsy's bed every night. His boyish charm makes me forget that he is the same man who whips Topsy and succumbs to her quaint fantasies.

'I hope you don't mind showing Inder around,' Bilal says. 'He's here for another two weeks and Topsy and I were running out of ideas for places we could show him in the city. Plus, we're off to Lahore tomorrow for a day.'

He winks at me and chugs a sip from his can of beer.

'Sure thing, it's always a pleasure to screw around with a fellow journalist.'

Bilal flings his beer can on to the ground and beats it slender with his shoe. 'Just don't do something I wouldn't do.'

I wink at him. He gazes at me slightly longer than he should, with a gaping mouth and wide eyes, as if I were a *bhuni hui rann*. I look away and spot Topsy walking towards us in the arms of a buff, bespectacled man who is clad in a grey suit and blue tie.

'Tanya, this is Indrajeet ... Inder,' she says. 'He's a visiting journalist from Delhi.'

'Is that right?' I hold out my hand for him to shake. 'And what exactly is a visiting journalist?'

'A travelling wayfarer, milady,' Inder says and kisses my hand. 'A man who's on a mission to find the truth.'

'Ah, so you're just bumming around?'

This sweet-talker might be tall and handsome, but he clearly has a lot to learn. He can't impress me with meaningless words.

'That's my Tanya, always full of wisecracks,' Topsy says, patting me on my back. 'Inder is in Pakistan to research sentiments on the insurgency in Kashmir.'

'Do you still think I'm bumming around?' Inder asks, sounding almost defensive.

'Well, I'm just glad about one thing,' I say, noticing his eyes light up with vague expectation.

'*Ah-han*, and what would that be?' The cheerful ring in his voice begins to irk me.

I'm tempted to do to him what I should have done to Saad. Or, for that matter, I should contemplate a more lethal strategy since Inder is a stranger and is making a special effort to act big and think small.

'I'm glad you flew down to assess the damage of your own government's policies in Kashmir.'

The poisonous words tumble out of my mouth and wipe the smile from his face. Topsy winks conspiratorially at me, as if my spontaneous remark was scripted and she knew all about it. Bilal clicks his tongue in disapproval.

Stunned into silence, Inder lowers his head and lets out an exasperated sigh. Moments later, he looks up, chortles and slaps his thigh.

'Spare me the barbs, milady,' Inder replies. 'I'm not the government. I'm just a wayfarer, a mere victim of circumstance.'

'You know, Inder narrowly escaped getting mugged today,' Bilal interrupts in an attempt to salvage his friend's declining reputation. 'I guess some things will never change in Karachi – with or without the MQM.'

'Is a mugging attempt your only claim to victimhood in a hostile country?' I ignore Bilal's comment about the MQM and stare into Inder's eyes in disbelief. 'If that were the case, I have already mastered the art of being the injured party in at least three countries.'

'Is that right?' he says, the glimmer of a smile appearing on his face. 'Tell me more about your escapades.'

'Last month, I got mugged outside Khadda Market,' I tell him. 'The thief, who tied a filthy kitchen cloth around his nose and mouth, was generous enough to take my CNIC out of my purse before I surrendered it to him.'

'One doesn't come across such a considerate *mugger* very often,' Inder says, his smile growing wider.

'You have no idea,' I respond wryly. 'He was so considerate that I was tempted to dupe him just for being so bloody inept at what he does. I managed to pull out my MasterCard and gave him a bag crammed with my sanitary pads, a deodorant and a hairbrush.'

My words bring roars of laughter from Topsy and Bilal. Inder continues to smile, as if he hasn't registered my joke and is concentrating on something else on my face.

'I wanted him to take my Mac lipstick as well,' I continue. 'But, *chalo*, as long as his wife is happy, I've done my part to close the socio-economic gap and fulfil my delusions of being Robin Hood's Pakistani love-child.'

Finally, Inder breaks into laughter, and I feel gratified.

'But it's terrible that you were mugged,' I continue. 'How'd you manage to escape?'

'I ran,' he said, laughing loudly as if he's cracked the funniest joke in the history of comedy. Topsy and I stare blankly at each other.

'Did he point a gun at you?' Topsy asks, mock concern creeping into her voice.

'Yes, a pistol.'

'As long as it's not a pellet gun,' I respond, sipping my drink. 'Those babies can blind you with one shot. I'm sure you know.'

'Touché.'

He gazes at me in anticipation, as if he waiting for my next assault so we can continue our light banter.

'Come on guys, don't talk about all this,' Bilal says, a sombre look on his face. 'Inder, I hope you didn't mind what Tanya said?'

'Nonsense,' he replies. 'In fact, I quite like her. *Ab ki baar, sirf Tanya se pyaar.*'

'Does he expect me to be flattered by this?' I whisper into Topsy's ear. 'If slogans were meant to be pickup lines, I'd be the first to turn Trump's "Make America Great Again" into "Make America Date Again" or ensure that everyone has access to roti, *kapda* and a hunky jawan.'

'Is that your way of defending Modi?' I ask, turning to Inder as Topsy sniggers into the palm of her hand.

'No, it's my way of asking if you'd like a drink.'

'I can get my own drinks, thank you.'

'I know. I like a girl who can call her own shots. Do you want to collaborate on my story? I'll give you full credit.'

'Are you offering me a job?'

At this point, Topsy and Bilal scuttle away in an ill-disguised attempt to give us some privacy. Moments later, I see them clicking a selfie with a frazzled-looking Mopsy and a harried Saad.

'Well, it's not so much a job as it is a request for assistance,' Inder says.

'I would have loved to,' I say, making every attempt to sound demure. 'But I'm awfully busy and I doubt my employer would appreciate my collaborating with Indian journalists.'

'Ah ... I see.' Inder seems disappointed. 'If you ever change your mind, you can write for our publication, *Time and Beyond*. We're always looking for opinions from across the border. Here's my card.'

'Why not get that TV anchor of yours who chides people on his show to write something?' I quip as I place his card into my Louis Vuitton bag.

'We're trying to look beyond the madness, you see. We are responsible for the future of our country. Twenty years down the line, our children will think we were mad to fight wars over a strip of land.'

'Aww, you are a closet Kashmir liberationist, aren't you?'

He sips his drink and moves towards me.

'Why don't you come closer and find out?' he whispers into my ear.

I've never met someone who can use a long-standing political crisis to get some action. Unless, of course, Topsy has tried this trick and not told me about it.

'Let's dance.' Inder tugs my hand and drags me to the dance floor.

10.50 p.m.

'So you think your PM's statements about Balochistan and Gilgit-Baltistan were premature?'

I yell these words into Inder's ears so he can hear me through the blaring music.

Inder shakes his head, flashes a smile at me and holds my hand , pulling me off the dance floor. My heart races with anticipation as we walk towards a dim-lit corner of the venue.

I notice Saad staring surreptitiously at us. He pulls away from Mopsy's embrace and the clutch of enthusiastic relatives and follows us out of the chalet and into a secluded corner of the car park.

I guess he is driven by a voyeuristic fascination for a woman he once slept with because he stands behind a neem tree and watches with relish as Inder buries his lips into my neck. Saad's face wears a despondent look, and the pain that shines in his eyes excites me more than the flower-soft caress of Inder's lips on my skin.

Am I slowly turning into Topsy? Does someone else's heartbreak – or lustful stare – serve as nothing but an aphrodisiac? I guess it was inevitable that at some point I was going to fall prey to some kink or the other. Though I wish it was an acceptable quirk. Like a foot fetish or something.

13 September 2016

12.30 a.m.

'Tequila or martini?' Topsy holds her glass in the air as if to inspect its contents. I watch her while munching on a plateful of rasmalai at the table next to the dance floor.

'Murree, not martini,' Bilal replies. She hits him playfully on his shoulder. Bilal laughs, moves closer towards her and pinches Topsy's chin.

I'm guessing this is a mild form of foreplay. Topsy has told me enough stories about their escapades for me to know that they're hardcore in the bedroom. I don't think I need a practical demonstration to enhance the listening experience. Fortunately for me, Topsy walks out of earshot and towards the dance floor with Bilal, her arm linked around his.

The guests are beginning to leave and the hum of chatter ebbs along with their departure. The dance floor looks strangely empty. Soon enough, Topsy and her Lahori hunk are the only ones who are foolishly dancing the Macarena as the newlyweds watch the performance, keeping time to the music by tapping their feet.

The bride whispers something into her husband's ear. Saad's face wears a pale, pathetic look. He keeps gawking at me from time to time. I don't understand why he's acting so prudish. It isn't difficult to guess that he wants to approach me, ask me about my brief encounter with Inder. But does he have to be so bloody obvious about his curiosity, I grumble to myself.

Inder left fifteen minutes ago. He promised to call me tomorrow. I know he won't keep his promise. I don't want him to either. I'll call him if I need him. If Inder is as smart as I think he is, he'll understand.

12.40 a.m.

My phone rings. It's Hafeez. I expect to feel guilt rush through my veins as his name appears on the screen. But at this point in the night, I'm much too satisfied in my drunken state to feel anxious. I answer the phone with a cheerful greeting, pretending as though nothing treacherous has taken place.

'How dare you!' an angry voice blares into my ears. 'I know Sonia hasn't been speaking to you. But did you have to do something like this?'

This is getting tedious. I wish there were better concerns in my life than Sonia and her broken engagement. It's difficult being labelled a bad woman when I don't even have enough feathers in my cap to be one. All my reputation has to boast is a drunken mistake (and, of course, attending Saad's wedding reception and getting off on his misery).

'How could you go to Mopsy and Saad's wedding reception?' Hafeez continues. 'Sonia will be very upset! You should consider yourself lucky that she isn't on Facebook.'

He always finds a way to figure out my darkest secrets even when I try to hide them. It's terribly annoying.

'It's all over Facebook,' he says. 'Someone uploaded pictures from the party. I saw you in the background of one of the pictures, talking to this muscular guy in a grey suit.'

I'm buzzing from the drinks I had but it's not hard to believe how easily I've been caught. The government should never use me as a spy, I would be discovered in no time. I'd find some way to leave behind clues and screw it all up. Because of me, Pakistan could go to war. I rein in my drifting thoughts and turn my attention, with some effort, to Hafeez's voice in my ear.

'Hafeez, please listen to me … you don't understand…'

What do I tell him? Should I tell him I came here for the free booze? He'd totally buy that. He knows better than to get in between me and my booze. But it still wouldn't be a good enough reason to betray my friendship with Sonia.

'Tanya, I don't want to hear any excuses,' he fumes. 'Carry on with your party. Go deceive a friend. Go talk to men in grey suits.'

'Hafeez, you make it sound like the man in the grey suit is bothering you more than the fact that I came to Mopsy's party.'

As I say these words, I immediately regret them. Unfortunately, I can't take them back. The damage has already been done.

'Tanya, seriously, I'm done with you,' Hafeez says. 'Don't talk to me. Don't call me. Don't even speak to me at work. You're selfish and frivolous. I don't understand what's wrong with you. What pleasure did you get out of sleeping with Saad? What pleasure do you get out of stringing these men along? You can't keep making men suffer because your father walked out on your mother.'

His words are like a slap across the face – and not the kind Topsy would enjoy. His cold voice brings tears to my eyes.

'Don't tell me why I do what I do,' I snap. I rise from my seat and walk towards the exit. 'You have no right to go snooping around like that. And I have every right to be at this party. It's not my fault that Saad left Sonia. It's not my fault that I was invited to this party. So what if I attended it and made out with Inder and got amazing booze?!'

'Ah, *Inder*,' the sardonic ring of Hafeez's voice makes my heart beat like a drum. 'I can expect no less from you.

I'm just glad you aren't sleeping with the groom again. You'd be mighty stupid to repeat that mistake.'

'That's it, don't ever call me again,' I respond curtly, digging my nails into the skin on my palms.

With that, I disconnect the call, wipe the tears from my eyes and decide to book a Careem home. If I get bludgeoned with an axe tonight, I'll at least have the satisfaction of having defended myself against the accusations made by people who I thought were my closest friends. I don't need Sonia's histrionics or Hafeez's views. I'd rather live on an island than be someone else's punching bag.

1.40 a.m.

'Khirad,' I whisper into the phone. 'Are you free to talk?'

Why am I calling Khirad at this hour? Has every sane and rational voice been suppressed in this city that I have to settle for second-rate opinions on my X-rated catastrophes?

'Oh yes,' she says chirpily. 'I was just thinking about you. I tried your Durex trick. It worked like a charm. But you say, what did you want to talk about?'

I tell her everything – from Sonia's engagement to Hafeez's unwarranted reaction. She listens in silence and, with time, I begin to think that calling her was probably not such a bad idea after all.

'Wow, this sounds messy,' Khirad says, clearing her throat. 'To be honest, I think Hafeez has a thing for you.'

'A thing?' For some reason, her words make my heart beat faster. I don't want to have murderous thoughts about him.

'Why, don't you like him? He's quite attractive.'

I think about all those times when Hafeez's views brightened a dull day into a meaningful one. But I don't want to share that feeling with Khirad.

'He's nice, but I don't really see him in that way,' I tell her firmly.

'*Chalo*, don't worry so much,' she says. 'Those who want us around will go to all limits to be with us. Go sleep. Tomorrow is Eid. You have to turn a new leaf. There's no point crying over people who throw shit at you.'

Khirad's words resonate within me even after she puts the phone down. Their soft cadence lulls me into a warm, dreamless sleep.

Kiss and Breakup

13 September 2016

11.30 a.m.

I wake up to a peculiar text message from an unknown number that makes me cringe with fear.

'*Bakri qurbaan hui, darling tere liye,*' I read the SMS out to Mummy as she sips her seventh cup of tea for the day. 'Do I laugh at the absurdity of the joke, feel flattered that some idiot is devoting his Eid *qurbani* to me or have the number blocked?'

Mummy simpers and the folds of her sea-green sari rustle against the sofa.

'You aren't the darling referred to in this message,' she says as she adjusts her bouffant. 'God is. You know, there's a fine difference between *ishq-e-haqiqi*– the love between man and God – and *ishq-e-majazi* – the love between humans. It gets confusing.'

I nod, uncertain about how I should respond to her.

Mummy plucks out a pair of Peter Parker spectacles from her purse along with a red pocket diary in which she often doodles throughout the day. In a fit of wild inspiration, she begins reciting a poem – one of her own pieces that remain confined to a secret notebook.

Mere is qalam ka boj uthatay uthatay
Tere hathon main nishan par gaye
Is umarqaid mein rehtay r htay
Mere zakhmon ka koi wajood na raha

(Since you've borne the burden of my pen
Ink stains have appeared on your hands
As I live through this life sentence
My wounds have started to heal)

'Wah!' I say with some enthusiasm. I am perplexed by her desire to spout poetry when her daughter is being harassed by obscene text messages. 'If only you didn't waste time talking to Bina Hassan and fighting with Aunty Saira, you could have become an exceptional Urdu poet.'

Mummy's face goes red at the compliment.

'I'm serious, Mummy. All you need is some time away from your routine.'

Maybe I'll have her institutionalized. She can write poetry in the silence of her confinement, like Bahadur Shah Zafar did when the British exiled him to Burma.

'Well, you're right,' she giggles. 'Saira was telling me that I should spend my evenings writing at the Sind Club gardens.'

'*Ah-han*, and where will you go when Daddy dies a painful death in Step-Mummy's arms and your entry to the club also dies with him?'

'Well, *beta*, I'll always have the option of turning your room into my study,' a smirk appears on Mummy's face. She truly is my mother.

'Why aren't you dressed yet?' she continues, rebuking me. 'What if someone comes over? What will they say? Stupid girl is sitting around at home, looking unwashed.'

For little over a week, Mummy has been insisting that I wear a black sari for Eid.

Eventually I'd agreed to buy a ready-to-wear Sana Safinaz *jora* to please her. But I changed my mind after I came across something from another outlet. It's called a croquis. I highly doubt the creators can pronounce the name either. It's an elegant white shirt with a netted hemline and thread-embroidered neckline.

'You wore something similar last year,' Mummy complained when she saw it. 'I knew you should have bought something pricier.'

I wish someone could explain to my mother that a journalist doesn't make as much as an investment banker does. And, even if I did, I wouldn't spend my earnings on an expensive *jora* from Sana Safinaz. A trip to Milan or a destination wedding in the Maldives would be better options.

12.30 p.m.

I scan through the city edition of the *Daily Image,* guiltily skimming over the glaring typos that have slipped into the pages, and read the headline of my story. Whenever I get a byline, Hafeez rings me immediately after he spots my name on the page and demands that we drive down to Ghaffar Kabab House for a dhaaga kabab. He always reads the papers by 9 a.m. on regular days. On Eid, Hafeez wakes up earlier than usual and usually messages me after namaz. Once he returns home, he skims through the newspapers while gorging on parathas with fried eggs. But he hasn't messaged me at all today. I guess he is still peeved at me.

His lack of communication leaves me with a burning anxiety, a fear of losing a friend. But the memory of his harsh words continues to sting me, their acidic inflections a reminder of how our relationship has changed with that one phone call. So I'm not going to make the mistake of calling him up and begging for forgiveness. Though if I don't apologize, I wonder if he'll ever free me from blame. If he doesn't, I'll have no one to discuss politics with or check out in the newsroom when monotony sets in.

The one thing that has surprised me is his jealous rage. Why does it matter to him if I was with Inder? Is Khirad right when she says Hafeez is interested in me? Like most men, Hafeez enjoys making women speculate about things he is indecisive about. Even if he's buying time until his latent feelings evolve into strong emotions, he's wasting my time till he decides what he really wants.

1 p.m.

My phone beeps. It's a message from Sonia. My heart begins pounding with anticipation and the fear of confronting another friend.

I read her message. 'Wishing you a prosperous Eid Mubarak.'

Trust her to use 'prosperous' for Eid. She makes it sound like the festival is a business venture where one can make a million dollars by drawing *Eidi* from pointy-nosed relatives. I'm tempted to send her a snarky reply and call her out on her stupidity. But you never know what's going through her troubled mind these days. If I depress her with my humour, she could jump off the roof. I'm sure that will hurt her more than a snarky comment ever can. But that won't work in my favour either. Hafeez will find some tangential way of making it all only my fault.

I don't want to botch up this opportunity to rebuild an alliance with Sonia, though. For all I know, if she were to drop dead one fine day – in some bizarre, unanticipated manner – and I have to take over and report on health, I might need her contacts. A reporter without contacts is like a flock of helpless sheep without a shepherd. Does that sound biblical? Well, it is difficult to avoid a pious spur in matters of life and death – especially in the case of Sonia's boring life and death which will, hopefully, open new doors and windows for me. *Inshallah!*

I type out a message on my phone. '*Khair, Mubarak.* I'm so glad you messaged. I've missed you, Sonia.'

As I click the 'send' button, I feel instantly redeemed, as if I had been weighed down by a burden that has finally been lifted.

1.45 p.m.

I receive a reply from Sonia after what seems like an agonizingly long interlude. 'Oh sorry. That was meant for someone else. I don't wish husband-snatching bitches on Eid.'

As I read the message, my heartbeat quickens. A cold fear seeps into my bones and suddenly I feel breathless. Written words do hurt more than words spoken in a fit of rage. I type out a reply to the message, content in the knowledge that my words will prick her like a cactus thorn.

'In that case, you shouldn't be wishing Mopsy this Eid. She's the one who snatched your husband. Though he wasn't even your husband to begin with.'

It takes me close to two minutes to send it across. I keep reading it to see if I can tone it down a little. But it's the truth anyway.

Sonia's reply comes swiftly after I send the text. 'Saad didn't become my husband because of you. It was because of you that he even considered sleeping with that bitch Mehnaz.'

There we go again. I'm tired of hearing about my drunken mistake. No one blames Saad for flirting with every girl in town. It seems as though Sonia suffers from permanent amnesia when it comes to Saad's mistakes. I'm sure there are more women out there who can vouch for his vicious, philandering ways.

But no one is willing to say anything. Each time Sonia's wedding debacle is brought up, all eyes and fingers turn to me.

'Aren't you giving me a bit too much credit here, Sonia?'

I am genuinely pleased with my response. Although it sounds a bit sardonic, the message conveys my side of the story without relying on melodrama or on facts that have grown stale over time.

2 p.m.

I plug my phone into the power bank and place it on the dressing table. Why should I wait for Sonia's reply when I can focus on other things that are far more important? I haven't left her speechless in a long time. I don't know if I have won the argument. But it feels great to have silenced her, even if it was through a senseless battle.

I open my cupboard and pull out my diary from my college days. Its cover is coated in a film of dust – Lurch never cleans anything. I flip through the sallow, dog-eared pages and find the entry about Hans. The first sentence reeks of the follies of a teenage drama queen and makes me cringe.

'Sonia still hates me for going to Fez with Hans,' it reads in cursive black ink.

Have Sonia and I always been in stiff competition for the same man? Well, not exactly. In my defence, I had no interest in Hans to begin with.

He was a German exchange student. Sonia had always adored him. She even harboured fantasies of taking him to the Goethe Institute for a poetry reading. I still don't understand lovers and their preoccupation with poetry. It all sounds so corny and uninspiring. But what else could I have expected from a hopeless romantic?

Aunty Zeenat, Sonia's cantankerous mother from whom she inherited all her charming traits, did not allow her daughter to go to Fez with us. So I went alone, lying to Mummy about spending the night at Sonia's house.

What I ended up doing the entire night is another story altogether. Hans and I drove down to his hosts' house in KDA where he puked on an expensive Afghan carpet and nearly set his hair on fire while trying to fry pakoras for his 'South Asian princess' – a compliment that was soaked in far too much orientalism for my taste.

But I can't forget how Sonia squealed on me. Mummy – who had taken to sporting a hijab at that point in her life and did not skip a single namaz – cried for days after she discovered the truth. She found a cruel yet ingenious way of getting back at me. At the time, the memory of her separation with Daddy still smouldered in her heart. She had grown so accustomed to it that she would frequently borrow an ember from it to ignite even the most incombustible parts of her life. Since I was her daughter – and I'm desperately seeking evidence that disputes this cold fact – Mummy also found ways to burn me with the small flames from her past that had laid siege to her present.

'You're acting just like your father's mistress,' she told me.

Years later, when I met my stepmother under false pretenses, I took great offence to the comparison. Mummy's five-timing namaz excuse worked to her advantage in those days and she was spared my wrath. Though, if I were to take a broad view of things, she only escaped my ire at the time because all I could think about was how ruthlessly my friend had betrayed me.

'Why would you tell her, Sonia?' I asked her one day in the college canteen, more out of concern than genuine anger.

'Well, I don't know,' she said. 'Maybe because I was jealous of you.'

'Love, you're not missing out on anything by not being with Hans,' I had said. 'He's overrated. It's our *gora* complex that gets in the way, you know. In any case, he's bad in bed.'

'Wait, you've had sex with him?' Sonia rose from her seat with her arms akimbo.

'Yes, but as I said, not worth it at all.'

Sonia didn't say anything more. I suspect she didn't want her illusions of Hans as the poetry-spouting *gora* to be shattered. By taking away the wild fantasies that were hitherto unknown to her, I'd deprived Sonia of the opportunity to dream.

Now, as I leaf through the pages of my old diary after all these years, I realize that Sonia and I are still trapped in the same dilemma. This time around, I sampled her ex-fiancé before she could and found him to be unpalatable. How do I negotiate the moral territory in such a matter?

2.30 p.m.

Every Eid, Lurch's kitchen harbours secrets. No one is allowed to enter the premises while he cooks.

After the Chinese keema fiasco, I've lost faith in his cooking. But Mummy trusts him blindly – which, incidentally, doesn't say much since Mummy's vision isn't exactly reliable anymore.

'See, he manages to put together a decent meal,' Mummy says as we sit around the table for the grand Eid feast. 'He's made biryani, korma and zarda. What more can we ask for?'

'I'm surprised that he didn't use any of his distinct culinary expertise this time around,' I quip as Lurch pours a glass of water for me. 'Last Eid, he put honey in sheer korma to add a new flavour to the dish. It didn't turn out as planned, if you remember.'

'*Khair,* we all have the right to make mistakes in life,' Mummy says, spooning some biryani on to her plate.

'And yet, you gave him four thousand rupees for making an effort.' I grab the spoon from her and throw a dollop of biryani on to my plate. 'I love how you manage to take out the exact amount from your purse for him.'

'Tanya *beta,* charity doesn't always begin at home,' she says, her voice muffled by a spoonful of biryani. 'Plus, what's the point of having a daughter who earns if she won't be financially independent and buy her Mummy gifts? So all my charity goes to Maulana Edhi.'

'*Hai,* my aching back,' she moans suddenly, holding her shoulder and cocking her head against her wrist. 'When will my suffering end?'

'If you continue wearing those heels, your suffering will stop ... permanently,' I say, lowering my head and diving into my plateful of food.

She ignores my remark, takes a second helping of biryani with a smattering of korma and we eat in silence.

3.30 p.m.

When I return to my room, I run a comb through my hair and check my phone. Sonia has finally replied to my message. What took her so long? I ask myself.

I open the message.

'I know I am. But who else do I blame?'

Had it been anyone else, I would have relented after reading this message. But Sonia is always prone to using words as weapons. She weaves a foolproof plan to emotionally blackmail people. She has become so adept at it that I think she doesn't even realize when she's doing it. So, despite the undisguised pain in her words, I am reluctant to let her win the argument.

I respond. 'Why do you need to blame somebody?'

5 p.m.

'Tanya?' Mummy storms into my room as I prepare for my siesta. Her sari rustles and her jewellery clinks as she walks in and sits on the sofa. Why is Mummy so dolled up anyway? Why does she have to dress up for every occasion, even if it is a trip to my room to disrupt my sleep?

'What's wrong, Mummy? I'm trying to sleep.'

'Don't sleep just yet,' she says as I roll about in bed and hide underneath the covers. 'Bina left that boss of yours.'

I sit up in bed and stare wide-eyed at Mummy.

'What? When?'

'Apparently Hassan was having an affair with some girl he knew,' Mummy continues. 'The girl sent a package full of condoms to their house with an unsigned letter telling Bina about the affair. What is worse, she told Bina that her husband has syphilis. Bina *toh* ran with the children to her mother's house in Lahore before Hassan could return home from Eid namaz.'

I must admit that Khirad has put this whole plan together quite well. But doesn't she fear getting caught?

5.20 p.m.

'Nonsense,' Khirad tells me over the phone. 'The man has way too many girlfriends. He'll never think it was me. Besides, I didn't tell Bina that I work at the *Daily Image*. I'd be rather stupid if I did.'

'Still, Khirad,' I say in a groggy voice that I am still silently cursing Mummy for. 'I'm glad you took this step.'

'Well, I did want him to get into trouble, but I never thought she'd actually leave him.' Khirad says, sounding bemused.

'So do you want to be with him now? You know, now that he's separated from his wife.'

'No, there's too much bad blood,' she replies. 'I don't think I can. He's difficult as hell and only likes to whine. And those idioms, *Allah maaf kare.*'

I laugh. Sonia could use a lesson or two from Khirad about how to deal with vile men and their idiosyncrasies.

Love at First Bite

15 September 2016

6.30 p.m.

Ipluck out my paperback copy of *Giovanni's Room* from Mummy's bookshelf. Most of the cabinets and shelves in the house are crammed with dusty, mildewed books that give off a musty fragrance that my mother, for some reason, claims is her natural scent.

But this book is special and doesn't deserve to be stacked next to Mummy's endless volumes of *Sachi Kahaniyan* and *Reader's Digest*. Adam had gifted this book to me as a school-leaving present. The book, which explores the turbulence of an American man's passionate gay relationship with an Italian bartender, was Adam's way of coming out to me.

Over the years, the truth of his sexuality has brought us closer. But lately I've involved myself in worthless friendships that have only increased the drama quotient in my life and made me want to bludgeon someone with an axe. Nowadays, I only see Adam at restaurants and coffee shops with uninspiring women who think they can woo his artistic fervour and become his muse. All of them resemble groupies – the kind of people who only go to PTI rallies to meet Imran.

Our friendship has been reduced to spotting each other, waving and going over to one another's tables to exchange platitudes. We occasionally text each other to catch up. But I miss our thought-provoking discussions. Unlike Sonia and Hafeez, Adam never judges me for what I do.

I should reconnect with him. What's there to lose anyway? I've already lost my nose among my friends. I guess I could also do without an index finger or a thumb if this plan backfires.

As I skim through the paperback, I dial Adam's number and pour myself a glass of Coke.

He sounds a little frazzled over the phone.

'What's wrong?' I ask.

'Oh nothing, just boy trouble.'

'Do you want to come over for dinner and talk about it?' I say. 'Mummy is going to meet a distant relative who feigns interest in our lives just to get access to gossip. And Lur ... the cook has been given the night off to celebrate Eid with his children.'

'You make it sound like privacy is a rare commodity in your house,' Adam giggles.

'You have no idea,' exasperation seeps into my voice. 'Mummy always insists that I accompany her to visit her relatives. Do you remember Aunty Mimi? Mummy's bossy cousin who belches more than she can eat? She parades me around her judgemental, jealous family like a *qurbani ki bakri*. So if you come over, I'll have a good excuse to not go.'

'Ah, Mimi. Is she the one who introduced you to that businessman last year? What was his name? Ahmad? Asim?'

'Ahmar, if I remember correctly,' I say as the memory returns to me. 'Anyone with half a brain could tell that he was a sleazeball.'

'I guess your Aunty Mimi, in all her effervescence and fake charm, hadn't realized that a good man's worth can't be measured by his bank balance,' Adam says. I laugh. 'She's still reeling from the shock of what I told one of those boring men she introduced me to at her dull party last month. He asked me what I wrote about at the newspaper and I went on this spiel about the need to write about menstruation without being embarrassed. Aunty Mimi's jaw dropped. The man smiled politely and walked away. I guess I was far too much of an embarrassment to be caged in a kitchen and strutted about like a trophy wife.'

'Why did you pick that topic?' Adam asks, amused by my boldness. 'Didn't Aunty Mimi pull you aside and pinch your arm? Or at least hit you on your forehead for acting smart?'

'To be honest, he seemed like the sort of guy who'd react badly to sensitive situations,' I tell Adam. 'But I wasn't sure, so I thought I'd gauge things for myself.'

'I guess you judged him well.'

'Haven't I always said that I can **read** men like they're primary school textbooks?' I say. Adam scoffs but promises to show up within an hour.

7 p.m.

'Adam is coming?' Mummy's harsh voice tears through my eardrums. 'Then it's okay. You can stay home and entertain him. I'll go on my own.'

For some time now, Mummy has felt sorry for my gay friend who was always on, what she believes, the fringes of society. She wasn't like this before. When we were children and Adam would come over to play, Mummy always said there was something *strange* about him and would insist that I stay away from him. I'm relieved that Mummy has finally been able to eject those homophobic thoughts from her mind. Unfortunately for both of us, other insecurities have taken their place, but one battle at a time.

'*Waise*, your friend should be careful,' Mummy says. She's watching an old Bollywood movie on DVD while sipping a cup of masala chai, which Lurch had brewed for her on special request. 'Look at what these terrorists are capable of doing. They'll get the gays next.'

Just when I think Mummy has broadened her horizon, she'll find a way to sound backward with her *bakwaas*. But her predictions have this rare, vociferous quality that makes them seem believable. One would suspect that she had heard all this straight from a terrorist's mouth.

'Yes, Mummy,' I sense the upcoming sarcasm in my tone and make no attempt to keep it under check. 'That's exactly what terrorists do now. It's the new fad, you know. Target the gays. Spot one, kill one.'

'Don't take all this lightly,' Mummy says, lowering the volume as a dusky Zeenat Aman, sporting hipster glasses, appears on the screen, lip-syncing to 'Dum maro dum'. 'They can strike at any point.'

Disgusted by Mummy's hypothesis, I walk out of the room. As I'm walking up the stairs, Mummy croons an improvised, croaky version of the song on TV. Anyone who expects Mummy to sing like Madam Noor Jehan will be hugely disappointed by her failed attempts to perfect a high note. But it is Mummy's choice of words that adds an element of surprise to the song. At that point, her singing prowess becomes a forgotten ordeal. Her improvised lyrics fill the air and make me cringe with terror.

'Bomb maro bomb, mit jaye hum. Bolo sobhoshaam, Taliban, Taliban.'

I knew I could trust Mummy to come up with an anthem, even if it is for a suicide bomber. She can be funny when she tries to be. If only she were less stingy and did something to exorcise those narrow-minded demons that lurk in her mind.

8 p.m.

'What do you mean he isn't sure about you?' My voice is tinged with mock surprise. But I doubt Adam realizes it as he takes a ravenous bite of the thin-crust pizza I ordered for dinner. He's started putting on weight. His double chin reminds me of the 'before' section of a weight loss ad.

'Stop eating so much!' I chide him. 'You'll go from looking dapper like Imran to being plump like Nawaz.'

'Do I detect a soft corner for the PTI?' Adam asks, biting into the pizza.

'Don't change the topic. Now tell me, what's wrong? Why is Ibrahim so uncertain?'

Adam wipes his lips with a tissue and gulps down another sip of Coke before he answers my question.

'Do you remember how difficult it was for me at Grammar School?' he asks, staring wistfully out of the window. 'I'd spend the games period sitting on a bench, reading Chaucer and chewing gum and getting yelled at by the games teacher for hanging out with the girls. What was the woman's name again?'

'Sima Butt,' I say. 'How could I forget? She was an unfortunately-named bitch who insisted on making me run laps.'

'Do you remember how the boys called me a homo with no mojo?' Adam diverts the conversation back to himself. 'And how the same boys would have their way with me in the secrecy of the locker room?'

How could I forget? But I thought Adam had put his past behind him. Now that he's dabbling in the arts, he's become quite abrasive. I thought this new confidence had ironed out the creases from his school days.

'Well, it's happening again,' Adam says, munching on another slice of pizza. 'Ibrahim says he's straight even though he touches me thrice a day. He's not sure if he wants anything serious. He thinks we need more time.'

Chalo, that's a fair demand. Adam has a tendency to frighten people. As an artist of some repute, he is known · for the emotional intensity with w   h he fills the canvas with colours. But no one seems to ppreciate it when Adam shifts this fervour from his paint gs and uses it to

navigate human relationships. When he is in this frame
of mind, he doesn't need to wear a Halloween costume
to make a person's blood turn cold with fear.

'How'd he reach this conclusion?'

'Well, after he realized that he's being bullied into an
arranged marriage by his parents.'

'What? With a woman?'

I know that's a silly question. If Ibrahim were daring
enough to marry a man, he'd get nothing short of 377
lashes. Not that anyone has ever been lashed or, for that
matter, stoned for this. But it seems like one of those
Topsy-like penalties that makes people want to flout the
law to reap the rewards.

'Yes, a woman,' Adam's shrill voice wrenches me
out of a complex web of random thoughts. 'She's some
cousin of his.'

'Oh, don't worry,' I say. '*Allah aur dega.*'

'And He did. Remember that Shia boy?'

'The one who wanted to take you to a *marsiya*?'

'Yes. Mohib and I met a few times. Then, one night
at a party, he got knackered and pounced on me. I didn't
mind initially. But then, he became a little too aggressive
and ... umm ... he bit my hand. It felt like a rat bite.
Honestly, I wanted to whack him and get tested for
rabies. But I guess I found it endearing too.'

Oh great. Another person in my life seems to have
implicitly sought inspiration from Topsy. Why can't
I have friends with simpler lives and easy-to-manage
problems? All these thoughts are beginning to scare me.
I think I need a smoke. Maybe the fumes of a burning
cigarette will choke Adam to death and I won't have to

listen to a long diatribe about the gay world in Karachi
and his boring Grindr escapades.

'So you like him now?' I ask, lighting a cigarette.

'*Naaa* ... he's just a friend. I can do way better. But I
think I like it.'

'Be careful what you say, Adam,' I say, laughing. '*Jhoot
bole, Mohib kate.*'

Adam guffaws and also lights a cigarette for himself.
I notice the creases on his forehead disappear as a smile
returns the glow to his face.

9.30 p.m.

'Hafeez is clearly interested in you,' Adam says, chugging
Coke straight from the can and turning his attention to
my problem.

'I love how everyone thinks that that's the only
explanation for his behaviour,' I reply, pulling the can
away from his mouth and gulping down its remnants.
'Maybe he's genuinely trying to protect Sonia from my
wretched, uncompromising ways.'

As the words leave my lips, I feel the uncontrollable
urge to laugh. I doubt Hafeez has any reason to protect
Sonia from me. He knows what she's capable of and will
certainly not endorse Sonia's misdemeanours any more
than he would endorse mine.

This Hafeez situation is getting rather mind-boggling.
Maybe Adam and Khirad are right. I guess I'm the only
airhead who doesn't understand his intentions.

'Hafeez's anger stems from fears and sentiments
which even he cannot comprehend,' Adam says.

'And what about me? Do I understand them? Or am I as clueless as he is?'

'You seem to have a better grip on things than he does,' Adam answers after a reflective pause. 'Though there's a lot that still needs to be said and done.'

10.15 p.m.

My phone rings minutes after Adam leaves.

'Hi, Tanya,' a hoarse voice says over the phone. 'It's Inder. Remember me?'

For some reason, the only recollection I have of the night I met Inder is Saad's voyeurism. The memory resurfaces in my mind and stays there till Inder's voice breaks my reverie.

'I read your story two days ago in the *Daily Image*,' he says in a gruff baritone. 'It's remarkable how you managed to tackle such a sensitive issue with panache. History is taught at Indian schools in more or less the same way.'

'Thanks for reading it,' I say, unmoved by his compliment.

'I was wondering if you'd like to meet on the 16th,' he asks in earnest. 'I'm going to this boring party at Mrs Palejo's house. She's a dowager whose husband left her a house in PECHS as compensation for cheating on her throughout their marriage. Sounds strange, no?'

'On what planet?' I blurt out the words and notice that the pitch of my voice has gone up a notch. 'I want to live that kind of life.'

'So do I take that as a yes? I just wanted to catch up and finish our unfinished business before it's too late.'

'If I say no, the business will remain unfinished. And so will you.'

Now I genuinely think there's something wrong with me. It seems as though I'm having one of those out-of-body experiences and Sonia has taken over my body to exact her revenge. There is no other explanation for why I sound so cheesy.

'I'm glad. See you tomorrow,' Inder pauses for oxygen. 'Just want you to know, you're truly something.'

Inder signs off the very next moment, as if he's much too shy to continue the conversation or thinks consent is a one-way street with no U-turns. *Khair*, I shouldn't be so judgemental about all this. I doubt he wants to opt for something serious with me – I can see through such overtures. But I admire his courage. It's refreshing to see that in a man for a change – even if it is a little frightening.

In any case, Inder might be my portal to new prospects. Maybe I could travel to India. Mummy could visit the country too to meet all her favourite Star Plus actors. Maybe I could take her to Agra. I hear there are some great mental asylums there. She could write poetry about the Taj Mahal's alabaster beauty. It's a lot better than rotting in a prison in Burma or sitting at Sind Club until Daddy dies.

11 p.m.

My phone beeps again. This time, it's a text message from Hafeez. My heart begins to race as I open it.

'Is it wrong that I already miss you?'

Ten seconds later, another message arrives and jabs me with its undisguised vulnerability.

'Don't hate me, Tanya. Picking you up in ten ... I'll honk when I'm outside.'

Hafeez needs a lesson in modern-day etiquette. People don't honk when they're outside someone's house. I doubt Daddy honked when he picked up Mummy for a date in the old days when antique telephones were the norm, PTV was the only channel on television and General Zia was still dredging up his dangerous alternatives to democracy. I'm sure Daddy had the decency to knock at her door and endure a severe reprimanding from Nana. And Hafeez wants to honk outside the gate to summon me!

I read the messages several times over until my fears finally subside. I want to reply but all I can come up with is a curt, unemotional response. 'Okay. See you then.'

I read the text several times after I send it, hoping that it can translate in a way that is more intimate and familiar. But I guess that's the best Hafeez will get from me after all those nasty things he said the other night.

And, if Khirad and Adam's superior wisdom is anything to go by, Hafeez needs to be honest about his feelings. He can't keep hiding behind Sonia. And he's really got to stop wearing those *purani* jeans.

Dhanno and the Indian

September 15

11.30 p.m.

Hafeez and I drive down to Seaview Road in stony silence. Usually when he picks me up for a late-night ice cream binge, we drive around the city in his blue Alto. The car – which Hafeez lovingly calls 'Dhanno' – has, with time, become a character in our friendship. As Dhanno would ply the potholed streets of Karachi – from Do Darya and Clifton to Bandar Park and Keamari – the rumble of her engine provided the background noise for our endless discussions on politics. When we were talking about people, Dhanno would squeak along, as if to contribute to our gossip session. When our conversation would lose momentum and Hafeez would switch on the radio and croon old songs in his gruff voice, Dhanno would fall silent and provide an audience to him. Meanwhile, I'd frown as he'd hum and butcher the lyrics of the song with reckless abandon.

But today, Dhanno is unusually quiet. Hafeez hasn't even switched on the radio. His silence is a painful reminder of the subtle shift in our relationship.

When Hafeez is angry, he makes it a point to vent his frustrations and make a production out of his emotions. Whenever he does this, I'm reminded of the days when Mummy and Daddy used to fight in their room while I'd cover my ears with my headphones and listen to Abida Parveen – of all people– to drown out their screaming voices.

But I'm much too preoccupied to obsess over his silence. From the time I left home, I've been bombarded with text messages from Inder. The steady flow of the conversation doesn't frighten me. In fact, I find myself strangely entertained. The man has an incredible sense of humour and has a witty, bitchy streak that leaves me giggling.

His latest text is honest, if not altogether tactful. 'I'm just saying that we should fuck till we drop. Everything deserves a shot. I just had one right now.' As I read the message, a question forms in my mind and I ask it without any hesitation. 'What kind of shots are we talking about?'

Within seconds, my phone beeps and Inder's answer is emblazoned on my screen. 'Gun shots, what else do you get in this *sheher*?'

I smile as I read his text, trying to suppress the urge to laugh. It doesn't bother me that an Indian has dissed my city. My patriotism has nothing to do with India, you see. But Hafeez is different. His jingoistic fervour borders on a fatal *junoon*. It's terrifying.

He notices my treacherous smile, stops the car and turns to face me.

'What's so funny?' he asks, sounding irate, like a child who has been excluded from an inside joke by his friends. 'Do share.'

'That's the first thing you've said to me after a perfunctory "hello" when I stepped into the car.' I look up at him, smile and put my phone inside my bag.

'That's not true,' he says. 'I suggested that we go to Seaview once we stopped at the traffic signal near your house.'

'That was me, Hafeez,' I laugh.

'Screw that. Tell me, what's so funny?' he nudges me, the memory of our fight forgotten. 'Who's making you smile so much?'

'Oh, it's just a friend I made at Mopsy's ...'

There are times when a seemingly innocuous remark throws you into more trouble than you'd expect to get into. I fear this is probably that golden moment for me.

'Is it that guy in the grey suit?'

'Umm ... yeah ... umm ... that's him.'

'I see,' he responds stoically. 'And do you speak to him often?'

'Off and on,' I say, trying to sound as non-committal as I can. 'He's a sweet man.'

'*Achcha,* so that's what been going on,' Hafeez's face contorts with rage. 'So that's what Tanya Shaukat does when she goes to her best friend's ex-fiancé's wedding.'

'Hey, that's not fair. I went because of Topsy, not because I wanted to spite Sonia.'

'You're lying to me, T.'

'I have always valued my reckless ability to lie, Hafeez.' I stare into his eyes. 'But I wouldn't waste a lie on something like this.'

'Do you expect me to believe that you are screwing that sweet man in the grey suit because of Topsy?'

Well, if we focus on the technicalities, Topsy did introduce me to Inder.

'What's his name?' he pipes up before I can respond to his last question.

'Inder,' I say, trying not to succumb to the burning desire to tell a lie. 'He's an Indian journalist.'

'What? Are you out of your mind? Why are you hanging out with an Indian journalist? Don't you realize how risky it can be in this day and age?'

'Don't be silly, Hafeez. He's a decent man. Don't say things about him when you know nothing.'

'Decent? *Haan*. How decent can he be?'

His scepticism reminds me of Aunty Saira's reaction when her other rebellious daughter Zehra, who studies at Wellesley College, convinced her American classmates that '*Kuch kuch hota hai*' was the national anthem of her 'home country'. When Aunty Saira came to know about her daughter's prank, she said what any god-fearing, patriotic Pakistani woman would say. 'If you wanted to fool a bunch of *goras*, couldn't you have chosen a nice Pakistani song instead? Why did you choose an Indian song?'

'Why do you care though, Hafeez?' I ask, my voice soaked in fury. 'It's my life. Not yours. Why do you need to pass judgement on the men in my life? Is there something you want to tell me?'

'Don't be silly, Tanya,' he says, scoffing as he pulls the key out of the ignition.

He throws open the car door and walks towards the bonnet. When he leans his body against it and lights up, I scurry out and stand next to him. He offers me a cigarette. I shamelessly pull it out of his hand, as if the urgency to smoke has erased the differences between us. We sit quietly on the bonnet for a few minutes and watch smoke rings swirl and disappear into the still air.

'You know, it's okay if you've developed feelings for me,' I tell Hafeez as I light the cigarette and take a drag. 'It's perfectly understandable. We're close. It's bound to happen.'

Hafeez stubs the last bit of his cigarette on the bonnet. Grey ash accumulates on Dhanno's blue skin. It resembles a line of coke, something that a cunning police-wallah, who is out to line his pockets during the Eid holidays by emptying out ours, could hold against us.

'Tanya, why are you so self-absorbed?' he responds defensively.

'I'm really not,' I say, flicking the ashes off the bonnet with the touch of a finger. 'I'm just saying. It's okay if you have feelings for me. You can tell me if you do.'

Hafeez sighs loudly and smiles wryly. 'And why would I do that? So you can go around telling people about my endowments like you did with Saad?'

'What?' I stare at him in disbelief, trying to subdue the anger growing within me. 'Where is this coming from? And, to be honest with you, men talk about women all the time. I don't see why you have to be such a hypocrite about this.'

'I'm the hypocrite?' Hafeez says, anger rising in his voice. 'You're the one who slept with your friend's fiancé and now want me to love you? Isn't that hypocrisy?'

'That's really not hypocrisy, Hafeez. You're just being judgemental.'

'I'm not,' he jumps to his feet, walks to the car door and roughly swings it open. 'I'm just stating facts.'

'And this is the point when I say goodbye.'

'Let's go,' he says as he sits on the driving seat and places the key in the ignition.

'No. I'll Careem it back. Don't worry about me. I'd rather get bludgeoned to death by a stranger than have you drop me home.'

'Tanya, don't be stupid. Come sit in the car.'

I walk over to the front seat, wrench open Dhanno's door and grab my bag. For someone who is terrified of entering a cab with strangers, I am putting on quite a brave face.

'Tanya, please...'

I slam the door shut, fish out my cell phone from my bag and hurriedly book a Careem.

'Why don't you understand, Tanya?' he asks, getting out of the car.

'Because I'm tired of being blamed,' I say without looking up to face him. 'I know I screwed up with Sonia. But that's between us. Why are you being so cruel to me? I didn't sleep with your fiancé. I slept with Sonia's.'

'Tanya,' he says, his hand tightening into a fist as he kicks Dhanno's tyre. 'I don't know. I really don't.'

With that, Hafeez gets back into the car, starts the engine, backs up and pulls away, abandoning me in the dead of night to wait for my Careem.

Sugar, Spice and Surgical Strikes

16 September 2016

11.35 p.m.

'All my husband did was sleep with his lousy secretary,' an inebriated Mrs Palejo tells her guests in the dusty drawing room of her house in Mohammad Ali Society. As the night progresses and the wine flows like a waterfall into her glass, she goes from smiling host to drunk woman struggling to form coherent sentences. Her lack of awareness doesn't stop her from holding up her wineglass and toasting the end of her strained relationship with her late husband. The dowager's drunken rage and fevered agony reminds me of the week Mummy spent in her room after Daddy announced his decision to remarry. Tears prick my eyes as the shards of that memory return to me. I blink them back and sip from a glass of chardonnay.

'I also come from a broken home,' Inder says in a husky, drunken voice. 'I can relate to your pain, Mrs Palejo, because I saw my mother go through it as well. My father used to beat her and it hurts me to this day.'

'So what?' I blurt out the words without thinking. 'It's no big deal. I also come from a broken home. I admit my father never hit my mother and only left her for another woman. But it's not my business. As long as I'm happy, who cares?'

Shocked into silence by my acerbic words, Mrs Palejo pours herself a drink and turns towards her other guests. I immediately understand that I will never be invited back to her house. I look at Inder, and I can see that he's disappointed. In whom? Me? Or Mrs Palejo, who is clearly being rude to her guest.

'Let's go, Tanya,' he says, his tone soaked in some unexplained sadness.

17 September 2016

12 a.m.

As we arrive at my doorstep, a smirk appears on Inder's face, as if he's recalling a comic moment from the past.

'What's so funny?' I ask as I rifle through my bag for the keys.

'You're adorable,' he winks at me. 'You can't hide anything from me. I could sense that Mrs Palejo's story rattled you a little.'

He moves closer towards me and pecks me on the cheek.

'You, like me, have been damaged by false relationships,' he says dramatically and holds my hands. 'I will cure you. Heal you from all those bad experiences.'

'The last thing I need is a saviour,' I reply and extricate my hands from his. I find my keys, open the door and wave goodbye. He turns around and walks towards the wrought-iron gate with a crestfallen smile and, possibly, a broken heart.

8 p.m.

'I don't know why I agreed to this double-date,' I fume to Topsy over the phone. 'Inder is clingy and keeps sending me text messages about how he wants to protect and love me.'

'Nonsense, *yaar*,' Topsy says, but I can sense her uncertainty and I realize that she might be second-guessing her plan of getting Inder and I together. 'Bilal will be there as well. We'll have a great time.'

'Well, I'm just telling you one thing,' I continue with my outburst. 'If he says anything weird to me, I'll ... I'll.'

'Relax,' she says. 'I'm sure it'll be fun. Don't form an opinion without at least going on a second date.'

'Yeah, because he'll magically transform into my perfect man,' I say with annoyance, but my tone softens. I guess Topsy has a point. I should stop being so prejudiced and at least give Inder another chance.

9.30 p.m.

During dinner at Café Flo, Inder holds my hand and refuses to let it go as he tells Bilal and Topsy about how fortunate he is to have met me.

'She's an angel, a work of art,' he says, his unclipped fingernails pressing into my skin.

'Is she now?' Bilal jokes. 'I always thought Tanya was a bit of a devil. You know, Rosemary's baby.'

Topsy laughs, takes a sip of her pina colada and observes my reaction with interest. The smirk disappears from her face as her eyes fall upon me.

'You're mistaken, my friend!' a giggling Inder exclaims. 'She's the woman of my dreams.'

Inder finally lets go of my hand. Beads of sweat have gathered on the back of my hand and I wipe them with a napkin and lots of hand sanitizer. As I look up, I notice Bilal staring at me. He winks. I smile back at him and turn away.

18 September 2016

8.30 p.m.

'The terrorists lobbed seventeen grenades at the airbase in Uri,' Inder says with the detachment of a newscaster as we drive to Fuchsia in Bilal's car. 'The gun battle lasted for six hours. Imagine what the soldiers went through.'

'It's terrifying,' I respond with an aloofness which comes from mourning a tragedy that is far too remote for me. 'If you want, we can cancel our dinner plans and head home.'

Topsy clears her throat to prevent herself from laughing.

'No, no, my princess,' Inder says, his sombre voice shifting to the shrill squeak of a cloying boyfriend. 'We're going to repeat the previous night's stellar performance.'

'Do you have tissues or sanitizer?' I whisper into
Topsy's ear. 'I have a feeling my hands will be clammy
with sweat.'

The moment we got out of the car, I beg Topsy to
swap places with me.

'Sure, darling,' she says with a sarcastic ring to her
voice. 'I'd do anything to sit next to your lover boy. As
long as he doesn't hold *my* hand. You know what I'd do
to him, don't you?'

'Do whatever you want to him at your own time,
Topsy,' I let out a sigh of relief. 'For now, just get him off
my back.'

9.15 p.m.

My decision to swap places with Topsy isn't entirely
sensible. As the waiter brings the starters, I sense something
crawling on my shoe and stroking my feet, its rough
texture piercing into my skin. I look under the table and
realize that Bilal is attempting to play footsie with me. I
roll my eyes at him. A lecherous smile floods his face as his
toes continue to rub against the skin on my feet.

Minutes later, his foot climbs further and travels up
my shalwar. It tickles in a good way but past experiences
compel me to handle the situation responsibly. I move
my legs away and sneer at him. He lowers his head, turns
to Topsy and passes her a plate of chilli garlic prawns.

11 p.m.

'Don't worry, Tanya,' Topsy says, seemingly unperturbed
by Bilal's behaviour under the table. I'm a bit shocked.

I know Topsy isn't overly possessive, but this feels a bit much even for her. She seems to have grown entirely liberated and willing to share. Sonia should learn how to not overreact from Topsy.

'I have an idea,' Topsy says, rather excitably. 'Use Bilal to ward off Inder. You have my blessing. I'll just speak to him after we fuck tonight. He'll totally be game.'

19 September 2016

8 p.m.

'Let me get the door for you, Tanya,' Bilal says. He pushes Inder aside and opens the door. Inder's face is flushed with irritation as we enter Mews Café. Bilal – who isn't even remotely apologetic about betraying his friend – escorts me to our table, pulls out my chair like a gentleman on heat, and sits next to me before Inder can occupy the seat.

'Let's order already,' Topsy says with a pretentious ring to her voice. 'I have a meeting with a bunch of lawyers at 9 p.m.'

She and I both know that there is no meeting with any lawyer.

'I'll have whatever Tanya wants,' Bilal says with a suggestive glint in his eyes.

'Excuse me,' Inder asks a waiter as he pours him a glass of water. 'Where is the lavatory? I'm not feeling too well.'

'Is everything all right?' Topsy asks with concern.

Inder eyes me like an abandoned puppy. I turn away and immerse myself in mindless conversation with Bilal. As Inder walks towards the toilet, his moccasins clank against the wooden floor as though they are protesting on his behalf.

9.30 p.m.

'But our electronic media has improved, no?' Bilal says. 'That's the only good thing Musharraf did for us. I tell you, Imran will revolutionize media as well when he gets the chance.'

Until we became partners-in-crime, I didn't realize that Topsy's beau was a PTI supporter. Topsy can't even stand the sight of Imran. How did she end up sharing a bed with one of his fans?

'Well, to be honest...' Inder says after what seems like an eternity of silence. 'I think India's electronic media...'

'*Meh*, India's different,' Bilal interrupts him, sidelining him with a gruffness that I didn't know he possessed. He turns to me and sniggers. 'Tell me more secrets about Pakistan's media, Tanya.'

Ever since Topsy left, Bilal's eyes have been transfixed on me. He has guffawed at my silly jokes as if I am the funniest woman on the bloody planet. Inder has observed us with a mix of anger and consternation and has downed three large bottles of water. In the course of one meal, we've tossed him out of our lives like damaged goods.

11 p.m.

Bilal insists on dropping me home. I don't stop him. As the three of us leave the restaurant, Inder comes closer to kiss my cheek and hug me goodbye. But I pull away, pat him on his back and follow Bilal to his silver Mercedes.

'Do you think we were a bit harsh with him?' I ask Bilal as he turns on to E Street. 'I wanted to get him off my back, not ostracize him.'

'Don't worry, he'll be fine,' Bilal says. 'Some men need to be shown their place.'

We make light conversation till we reach my house.

'Thanks for dropping me off and helping me,' I say and hold out my hand, expecting him to shake it. Bilal reaches forward, holds my wrist, strokes his fingers against it and kisses the back of my hand. I pull the car door open and scurry into the house before the situation escalates and the entire city decides to burn me at the stake for snatching another woman's lover.

11:20 p.m.

I ring Topsy and tell her about what Bilal did. Even though she's the one who suggested the plan, one has to be careful these days. Everyone is so possessive of their lovers and I don't want to endure the unpleasant effect of raw, jealous hostilities – not again. I'm not like Imran, who keeps proposing a *dharna* after a new cataclysm effects the game of dirty politics.

Topsy laughs when I explain how her Bilal kissed my hand and made me uncomfortable.

'I guess there's only one solution,' she says. 'Sleep with him.'

'Doesn't it bother you when he does these things?'

My question is a shameless attempt to pry into their personal lives, in the hope of understanding how their relationship works. It might just give me a ready-made excuse for all my indiscretions.

Topsy clicks her tongue, as if I've said something wrong or bigoted.

'What he does when he's not with me isn't my problem,' she says. 'If he behaves when he's with me, I have no reason to complain. The same rule applies to me.'

If only Sonia were as progressive as Topsy and understood that sometimes a flexible relationship works in everyone's favour, we'd still be friends.

29 September 2016

10 p.m.

Inder has sent me an email. It's peppered with a veiled apology and an offer.

'Let's put this behind us. I was wondering if you'd be interested in writing a piece for our publication about how the situation is in Pakistan after Uri and the current perceptions about violence in Kashmir. I was working on the story myself. But it's better if we get an insider's view.'

What is this? Is he trying to be generous so that I'd forgive him? Maybe if I ignore this email, he'll get the hint and leave me alone.

11 p.m.

But unwilling to accept a refusal, Inder sends me a text message to explain the details.

'We want to take a neutral stance,' he writes. 'We want the world to see beyond the madness over Kashmir. We want you to write about the reactions to the surgical strikes in Uri.'

When I ignore his message for a second time, Inder decides to call me instead.

'Don't be difficult, Tanya,' he says. 'I'm not asking you to write this piece as a former love interest. This is strictly professional.'

'I'm genuinely sorry for what happened,' I pause in anticipation for him to accept my apology but continue when his silence prompts me out of mine. 'But why do you want me to write the piece? Can't you find someone else who is interested? I'm sure you'll get a well-researched piece from someone with the right credentials.'

'But I want you to write it,' he lowers his voice. 'After I read your piece on the history textbooks, I knew you'd be the perfect person to write this story.'

Does he mean it? I can't tell.

'What are you thinking?' Inder's words penetrate through the quiet.

'I don't know,' I say, still mired in a web of puzzling thoughts. 'I've been meaning to write a gut-wrenching critique on the possibility of the Indian PM doing away with the Indus Waters Treaty. But...'

'Let that be your starting point,' Inder replies eagerly. 'What were you thinking of writing?'

I tell him about a conversation I had with Mummy last week, when rumours were flying thick and war seemed imminent.

'I insisted that we should use water sparingly in case the taps in our house run dry. I also suggested that we buy an extra can of water when we went shopping at

Agha's Supermarket yesterday. You never know when we can lose water, just like the hair on our heads.'

The image of an empty faucet and water shortage stirred by political conflict clearly excites Inder. His voice becomes chirpy, almost musical.

'I was expecting her to take this stuff seriously,' I continue. 'But Mummy had more pressing matters to consider, like her Indian TV channels being banned. How would she survive without knowing what happens to her Gopi *bahu*?'

Inder laughs haughtily.

'But see, these are elitist complaints,' he lowers his tone to a whisper, as if he were speaking to a child. 'What does the common man have to say about all this?'

His words make me suddenly self-conscious, uncomfortable in my own skin. The cold logic of Inder's words reminds me that a narrow lens never provides an honest glimpse, no matter how hard it tries.

'Of course,' I hurriedly respond. 'It will require a great deal of fine-tuning. I could throw in my city editor's casual misogyny about Mehbooba Mufti being a "puffy-eyed monster in a time of crisis". But I'll let you know if I can write the piece.'

'What are you concerned about? I'm sure you'll do a great job. And you'll get great exposure. I swear.'

'The word "swear" means two things in the English language, you know,' I retort. 'Which one are you going for here?'

He laughs, and then asks me if I'm in.

'I'll think about it.'

'While you're at it, think about someone else too,' Inder answers.

I pretend that I can't hear him and disconnect the line. Before I can heave a sigh of relief, the phone rings again. Hafeez's name appears on my screen and I answer the phone with a snappish, unwelcoming greeting.

'Tanya, I need to see you,' he says, his voice cracking with emotion.

'What's wrong?' my tone softens. The visceral rage I feel against Hafeez recedes and anxiety takes its place. 'Is everything all right?

'Just meet me,' he sobs. 'I need to see you.'

'Sure. Come over. I'll be here.'

Like most men, Hafeez is strange when it comes to crying. He is always outraged when anyone even insinuates that he cries, as if there could be no stronger assault on his manliness than to assume that he is sentimental.

So now it's very unusual to hear him weep over the phone. His pain disturbs me. I wonder what's troubling him? And why does he want to see me? I thought he couldn't stand the sight of me. Has he changed his mind again?

11.45 p.m.

Hafeez is sitting on the sofa in my room. Fortunately, Mummy is visiting one of her relatives and has not been lurking about the house. Lurch is probably in a dark corner of the kitchen, eavesdropping. Not like I can do anything about it, though.

'Is everything fine?' I ask Hafeez with concern. 'You sounded worried over the phone.'

Tears gush down from his eyes and moisten his cheeks. Hafeez takes my hand into his rough palms and moves closer to me. For a second, it looks like he's about to say something, and then, instead, his fingers clumsily travel to my shoulders, pulling me towards him. He presses my body against his, tilts his head and kisses me. I haven't been expecting this, but somehow, it feels like the most natural thing in the world. I give in, kissing him back.

A few minutes later, he wriggles himself out of my embrace, clumsily rises from the sofa and struts out the door. I follow him to the staircase and watch as he makes a dash for the front door. His movements are swift, as if his actions were prodded by a fear I cannot immediately understand. It is only after the latch of the door clicks into place that I realize that he is gone and the moment that subsumed my darkest fantasies is over.

I run a finger over the length of my upper lip, checking for traces of that intimate caress, but it's already fading. Already, what just happened is beginning to feel like a dream. I pull out my packet of Marlboro Lights and light a cigarette, observing how its fumes curl in the air. Minutes later, the smoke disappears but a smouldering scent hangs over the room – the aroma of an unsolved mystery.

Headlines on Deadlines

8 October 2016

11 a.m.

'The tragedy is that the anti-honour killing bill was an afterthought. It was introduced during the parliamentary session on Kashmir to deflect public attention from the ongoing conflict with India. This was what Jamshed Dasti Sahib was trying to say at the session.'

These golden words, tinged with unrestrained cynicism, fall out like a stream of saliva from the lips of a paan-chewing, Khaadi-wearing male social activist during a panel discussion at an event Hassan has sent me to, where a posse of 'experts' convey, quite weakly, their views on preventing violence against women. As I expected, the programme is appalling.

'That's not a fair comment at all, Qasim Sahib,' the voice of a male women's rights activist on the panel exclaims from the other end of the hall. 'Have we already forgotten what happened to Qandeel Baloch and all the other girls who have fallen victim to this cruel practice? This law is the need of the hour.'

'With all due respect, the new law will really make very little difference,' a third voice on the panel, a sari-clad woman who seems collected and composed, interrupts them. What we need are more specific laws.'

I sit in the front row and jot down some points in my notebook, cursing Hassan under my breath. I message Khirad in an attempt to unleash my frustration.

'This is the last time I'm listening to Hassan. I can't believe he sends me to cover such dull events.'

Khirad's response arrives swiftly. 'He's probably under stress after Bina threw him out with his luggage.'

As the panelists continue to bicker among themselves, I type a quick reply to her message.

'That's true, she's pinched out every penny from his pocket. But being her ex-husband-to-be doesn't absolve him of his professional responsibilities.'

Her next message shocks me with its unconcealed compassion toward her ex-lover. I guess Khirad's affection for Hassan was not causal, after all.

'But the poor man, can't blame him. He's been so upset, especially since I left the company and joined Gol TV.'

I thumb out another response while the men on the panel gang up on the lone woman.

'Yeah. *Waise*, at least this event has made me realize how journalism has made me a passive recipient of flawed ideas thrown around by other people.'

Khirad stops replying and I revert my attention to the panel discussion. As the clamour turns into a bitter war of words, I place my pen behind my earlobe and watch the argument unfold before me with indifference. I begin pondering over the ways in which journalism has killed the activist within me.

I text Topsy because she's known me through my rebellious years and has observed the boisterous dissident within me mellow out into a bored, overworked subeditor.

'I'm stuck at a discussion about the anti honour-killing bill.'

Minutes later, I send out another message, underlining my distress.

'In college, I'd be out on the streets shouting slogans and protesting, instead of passively watching impotent debates. What has happened to me?'

The absurdity of Topsy's response makes me grin with pleasure. 'You journalists are the new-age Grim Reapers, wielding the scythes of bad news.'

I grin as I type out my reply, ignoring the moderator's dull speech concluding the session.

'You make us sound sadistic.'

She texts back. 'Not at all. All I'm saying is that you need to break away from the GrimReaper effect. Cheer up, it's not so bad.'

The audience claps as the discussion comes to an end. The panelists bow like theatre actors do after a play. Once the trance of their onstage facade is broken, they talk cheerily among themselves, their disagreements forgotten. I rise from the chair and walk towards the entrance. Outside, it's another sticky October day. I can't believe I'm expected to write a report on this sham of an event.

1.30 p.m.

The smoking area at the office looks almost derelict. The people who would sneak out of their cubicles for a fag in the middle of the day seem to have gone into hibernation or, worse, have stopped smoking altogether.

Even Hafeez isn't here yet. Over the past few weeks, he hasn't said a word to me. The only time I've heard him speak is when he's chatting with Sonia, Hassan and the others at the office. His body language is the only way I can gauge his mood nowadays. While this gives me a reason to check him out more than I usually do, his silence towards me is infuriating and painful.

And honestly, I'm growing tired of these mixed signals.

2 p.m.

I return to my workstation in a bad mood. In search of a comfortable distraction, I check my phone to find that Sonia has left me a stream of messages.

Yes, the silence between us has slowly ebbed away. She started texting me again last week to inform me about story ideas. Like Hafeez, Sonia doesn't even bother to talk to me at work. And each SMS, curt and businesslike, makes me think of the mistakes I've made with Sonia.

Her first one was cold and succinct. Every word had been honed with a purpose, reminding me that I was an outsider, a stranger who no longer belonged to her world. 'Will be sending you a story on the new appointments made at government hospitals across the province.'

Today, her message sounds much more promising.

'They've swapped two newborns at Sirius Hospital. Parents are angry and have created a scene at the hospital.'

This is probably the first time in Sonia's uneventful career as a journalist that she's covering breaking news. I'm curious to know how she'll handle it.

But even though I doubt she'll do justice to the story, I send her a reassuring text message so she doesn't have another reason to despise me.

'Looking forward to reading your story, Sonia.'

2.15 p.m.

Hafeez walks into the newsroom and throws a sidelong glance at me. I look away, my eyes glued to my computer screen and my fingers clattering against the keyboard. As he nears his seat, I wait for him to turn around, smile and speak to me.

But he doesn't. I turn back to work, and I can feel his eyes on me, watching my every move. Over the past few days, I have realized that Hafeez is battling some inner demon. I can sense the longing in his eyes each time he looks at me. For Hafeez, Tanya Shaukat is a friend you kiss and never tell a soul about; a secret that is best left concealed.

I decide it's time for a cigarette break. There's a limit to which I can endure Hafeez's silence and his furtive glances. I have never been like this. Tanya Shaukat always knows how to approach a crisis with charming irreverence and without stepping back. But my spat with Hafeez has made me nervous of my actions, terrified of their consequences. I can only bury my feelings in a comforting cigarette.

2.30 p.m.

'Come have dinner with Bilal and me tomorrow,' Topsy tells me over the phone. 'We'll go to Sakura. Make a celebration out of it. You'll feel a lot better.'

Topsy always has a panacea for my problems. Whether it's through booze, free weed, boys or an awkward dinner, she's always got me sorted. Her calm and carefree demeanour provides a quick remedy for anything that's troubling me – which is more than I can say about Mummy's painfully nurturing ways.

'But what about Hafeez?' I ask. 'How will this help me deal with him better?'

'Honey, don't get worked up over a man like him,' Topsy says, sounding positively nonchalant as she comforts me. 'He's a dot on the windshield of your life. Flick it off or wipe it clean. You can't keep complaining about a speck of dust on a glass table when the rest of the table is squeaky clean.'

'You've become rather cerebral since Bilal decided to turn his efforts towards helping PTI topple the government, haven't you?' I attempt to distract Topsy with her own problems.

'I guess. I do tend to think more when the sex gets less exciting.'

'Have Bilal's standards fallen drastically?' I ask. 'Lost his focus in the bedroom, has he?'

'He's focusing his energy on politics, I guess. I'm trying to make my peace with it,' Topsy replies. 'That's democracy, you know. Sharing is caring.'

2.45 p.m.

Topsy's pep talk has eased my restlessness and I am finally able to be productive at work. As I approach the final sentence of my second edit in ten minutes, Hassan walks out of his office and leans against my desk. A grin appears on his face as his hands fiddle with a small stack of papers and pull out a document from the pile for me to read.

'This is a press release about an event organized for the eleventh anniversary of the 8 October earthquake,' he says. 'I want this to go on the front page. It's important.'

I skim through the document and realize that it has been sent by an NGO. Large chunks of the story have been devoted to the names of the organization's officials, along with their long designations.

'Hassan, this is a terrible press release,' I continue to skim through the document, aghast at the promotional nature of its content. 'It has nothing about the earthquake itself. They've squeezed the NGO's name into every sentence. How can this go on the front page?'

'Don't be silly, Tanya Bibi.' Hassan rolls his eyes and then grimaces. 'Of course it can.'

As Hassan returns to his office, I scan the document again and cringe at its shameless self promotion. I place it on my desk, open a Microsoft Word document on my screen and type out a fifty-word summary of the event that excludes unnecessary details.

'Sure, we'll use it, but he didn't tell me how to use it,' I whisper to myself and smile mischievously.

Hassan, I've discovered over the years, has many cousins and cronies sitting inside air-conditioned NGO offices. He never shies from giving them a space to flaunt their talent for deceit. His veiled agenda shamelessly inhabits our pages, hanging like an unwanted layer of flab that no measure of rigorous exercise can remove. I sometimes feel like the *Daily Image* is a PR company and I'm the spokesperson for Hassan's convoluted mind. So today, this spokesperson will do what she wants to do.

3.15 p.m.

My phone beeps with a text from Inder. 'Have you made a decision about whether you want to write the piece yet?'

I respond half-heartedly. 'I'll do it. As to what I'll say, that's a work in progress.'

'Work in progress, eh? Just like our love story.'

Seriously. This is an all-time low, even for him. Should I say something? Maybe I should threaten him into behaving by withholding my article. After all, withholding sex seems to work.

I ignore Inder's message and decide to call Khirad. She'll probably be at the hospital too since she now reports on health issues for Gol TV.

I rise from my chair to go to the smoking area. Hafeez cranes his neck and glances sideways at me. I throw a deadpan look back at him and he swiftly averts his gaze and looks at the television. He has been staring at me surreptitiously all these days. It is a secret exchange that I have grown accustomed to. Whenever he realizes that I have noticed him staring, he turns away, visibly chagrined at having been caught gawking at me.

But this time, Hafeez is distracted by a live news bulletin. A prim, black-suited newscaster – who bears a striking resemblance to Inder – reads out the hourly update. If eyewitnesses are to be believed, a female reporter has been slapped by a security guard at Sirius Hospital.

'Shit,' Hafeez hisses. 'They're talking about Khirad.'

Hassan runs out of his room and moves closer to the screen. I study his expression as the shock in his eyes is replaced by an unmistakable glint. Our city editor seems to derive a sadistic pleasure – a thrill from knowing that his former lover has been publicly ridiculed. It's terrifying to see his expression morph in front of my eyes. It angers me that he can be a chameleon when my friend has been affected. I rush to the smoking area to call Khirad.

3.40 p.m.

'What do you mean he slapped you, Khirad?' I demand in an annoyingly shrill tone.

'I don't know,' Khirad says, her low voice tinged with dread. 'I was trying to get the doctor's comments about the babies who had been swapped. The guard wouldn't let me into the ward. When I insisted on being allowed to enter, he called me a *kutiya* and then slapped me.'

Khirad's retelling of the incident appears to be somewhat dull, as if she has compromised on the essential details of the story. It doesn't pulse with raw energy and histrionics as I had expected it would. The way she narrates what should have been a traumatic – if not devastating – experience, makes me wonder about the pains taken by news channels to make a non-event seem all the more glitzy and significant.

'What are you going to do now?'

'I ... don't ... I should go talk to the press and clear this out. I'll talk to you later.'

3.50 p.m.

After I finish my cigarette, I return to the newsroom. Hassan is holding court at his office. Sonia has returned from the hospital and is narrating the story about Khirad with a harried look on her face. Hafeez is sitting next to her, his arm slung around her shoulder.

'I don't understand why he hit her,' Sonia says, still shocked by the incident. 'She only wanted to go inside the ward.'

'She deserved it,' Hassan suppresses a giggle. 'I hear she was asking personal questions.'

'How stupid of her to get herself into this mess,' Hafeez pipes in. 'Who told her to quit the *Daily Image* and join that channel?'

Instead of relying on a sensitive and reliable account of the incident – which can only come straight from Khirad's mouth – Hafeez and Hassan are churning out their own twisted conclusions. Journalists? Bah!

Sonia raises her head and then stares at the ceiling. I can tell she is visibly uncomfortable. Her eyes are her biggest giveaway. As I walk into Hassan's office, they look weak and weary.

'*Aao aao*, Tanya Bibi,' Hassan points his hand to an armless chair next to Hafeez as he sees me enter the newsroom. 'Come sit. Let's discuss the Khirad episode.'

Hafeez moves his chair closer to Sonia as I prop myself on the empty seat. I can hear his breathing – he's letting out a faint whistle from his nostrils that distracts me. It seems as though my presence is a source of discomfort for him because he starts shifting uncomfortably once I'm settled in. But I decide to ignore him, his body language and its hidden meaning.

I turn my head towards the television. Khirad is now on air, speaking to a TV anchor about what happened. But the anchor's constant probing and relentless nitpicking keeps interrupting her story.

'Don't you think you did the wrong thing, madam?' the anchor's voice resonates through the room. 'After all, he is a poor security guard who is doing his duty and you are a privileged journalist.'

'Privilege is the last thing you think of when Khirad comes to mind,' I say and turn away from the screen, irritated by the reporter.

Hafeez ignores me. Sonia adjusts her dupatta around her neck and heaves a sigh.

'But nowadays, few journalists are competent,' I say stoically. And even fewer can become surprisingly good friends over a hot cup of well-brewed chai, I think to myself.

I'm nervous as I wait for Khirad to respond to the anchor's harsh scrutiny.

'So, Tanya Bibi,' Hassan says, zapping the remote control at the television set to mute the volume just as Khirad begins to speak. 'You believe that Khirad is completely innocent?'

I stared at Hafeez, taking in his ripped, mud-stained jeans – he still wears such god-awful , shabby clothes – and Sonia turns to face me, waiting for me to defend Khirad.

'For some reason, ever since Khirad left us for Gol TV,' I hear myself say in a high-pitched voice, 'all of us seem to have become so condescending and cruel towards her.'

Hassan leans back in his chair and fidgets with a pen.

'At first, it was funny,' I point out. 'But as time has passed, the comments have gotten more and more cruel, and Khirad has basically become the target of malicious gossip.'

Hassan laughs. 'You know, she just got the job because she knew Gol TV's CEO,' he says. 'She has no real talent. Your friend has always taken shortcuts to get to the top.'

A sudden silence creeps into the office. Sonia lowers her head and distractedly checks her phone.

'I think that counts as slander, Hassan, doesn't it?' I say, wagging a finger in the air to show him that I mean business. 'She got slapped in public. And for what? For doing her job? For asking questions in the capacity of a journalist? We should stand by her instead of stabbing her in the back.'

'But Tanya Bibi,' Hassan waves his hands in the air and smiles. 'Who said we're stabbing her in the back? We are just saying what we feel.'

'But what you feel has no bearing on anything. If she chose to leave us for Gol TV, it's her prerogative. And who knows what her real reasons were?' I look pointedly at Hassan, whose smile wilts.

'Calm down, Tanya,' Hafeez says patronizingly. He clears his throat, as if to expunge any traces of empathy from his voice.

'No one is ganging up against Khirad,' he continues without meeting my eyes. 'I know she's your friend but ...'

He falls silent, turns his head and presses his thumbs against his eyelids and sighs. Sonia stares at me and smiles. Her silence fills me with unease and I'm tempted to call her out for not taking my side.

'Tanya Bibi,' Hassan says. 'Come, let it go. No point arguing. Let's all get back to work.'

Sonia rises from her chair and walks off. The faded smile returns to Hassan's face as he turns to Hafeez.

'Let's take this on the front page, okay?' Hassan's deep, authoritative voice rings in my ear as I leave his office. 'With a sensational *si* headline.'

'Why not?' Hafeez chortles. 'After all, Khirad is our former employee.'

Every story needs a villain. But even Brutus had the decency to be a backstabber. A front-page story will tarnish Khirad's reputation. And a pack of condoms won't be able to save her this time.

Tempest at the Temple

8 October 2016

4.45 p.m.

At home, I lie on the bed, close my eyes and dream of travelling to Bali or Phuket – any place to which I can go on a cheap airline ticket.

As I steadily descend into a much-needed slumber, Mummy knocks on my room door, wrenching me out of sleep.

'Mummy, *kya hai*?' I rub my eyes and roll over on my bed. 'Can't I get any peace in this house?'

'You want peace?' Mummy asks matter-of-factly. 'How can there be peace in this house?' Her voice is charged with emotion. Great, what new drama now?

'Why? Did Lurch burn your pakoras?'

'Nahi *beta*, he did something worse,' Mummy peeps out of the door and then shuts it. 'I found the DVD of an adult movie in the kitchen.'

I get out of bed and walk over to the mirror to fix my hair. Finally, a domestic squabble I don't want to sleep through. Mummy is pacing the floor, her face crestfallen. She's mustering the courage to confront her loyal servant. This is going to be fun.

'What movie was it?' I ask.

'Tanya, how can you worry about what movie it was? The point is that he was watching it in *our* home.'

'Chill, Mummy,' I say. 'Lurch is a lonely man. He probably needs something to feel content.'

'Tanya!' Mummy screams, visibly horrified that I have dared to consider Lurch to be a sexual being. 'We need to do something about it. We can't sit around and wait for him to hide the evidence.'

'*Tauba*, Mummy. It's not like he's killed someone. He was just having some fun. Must you be so judgemental? Besides, you're the one who got him a DVD player and TV for the kitchen. Stop being so prissy about the whole affair.'

'Fine,' Mummy says, tears welling up in her eyes. 'Don't listen to me. Who cares what I think anyway? I should just go drown in a *kua*. You and Haji will be happy then. He can watch his *gandi* films and you can support him.'

Ugh, Mummy has truly mastered the art of unbearable dramatics.

'Stop sulking,' I say. 'Let me come to the kitchen with you. I'll talk to Lurch.'

6 p.m.

'*Nahi, baby*,' Lurch snivels. 'God-promise, baby. I have no *gandi filam* with me. Please, Begum Sahib. *Baby ko samjhao na*.'

Mummy crosses her arms and turns away, as if she were Lurch's jilted lover, not his employer.

'Tanya, inspect his belongings,' she says, pausing between each word and enunciating each syllable to instill fear in her man Friday's heart.

'Mummy, I'm not going to go through Lurch's suitcase. It's probably filled with his smelly undies and sweaty *banyans*,' I protest.

'What do you mean?' she shouts. 'Don't you see what he's done?'

'I do,' I say, folding my arms against my chest. 'But checking his belongings is an invasion of privacy and I can't do that.'

Mummy is taking all of this a bit too seriously. So what if her cook turned out to be human? There's no reason for her to feel betrayed. She always finds new reasons for overreacting.

'I'm sure he hides his porn DVDs in the kitchen and watches them when no one is around,' Mummy wags her finger. 'Haji is, in all the most important ways, daft enough to do something like that. At least look for it over here.'

I can't say no to this request. With reluctance, I open each cabinet in the kitchen and rummage around.

'Now let's see where these videos are,' I whisper to myself.

Lurch wipes his tears with a *safai ka kapda*, doing his best to look innocent. Mummy watches me with eagle eyes as I forage for Lurch's porn.

6.10 p.m.

I've looked through the cabinets and drawers. All I found were knives and forks and my grandmother's fancy plates and bowls from London. Or was it Geneva? Anyway, who cares?

If I were a man who watched porn in a kitchen, where would I hide it?

6.20 p.m.

'Ah-hah,' I pull out a DVD from the baking oven. Did he think I wouldn't look there? I'm quite adept at finding things that don't belong to me. I'm Mummy's daughter, after all. Sleuthing and snooping are qualities I picked up in the womb and honed through my teens.

'*Hain?*' Mummy squeals at Lurch. 'What's this? *Razia ki Razai?* How low can you stoop?'

I inspect the DVD cover. A broad-shouldered woman gapes back at me from under her silk *razai*. I smile back at her and dispel the desire to laugh.

'Begum Sahib, please forgive me,' Lurch pleads.

'How dare you bring this trash to our house!' Mummy roars with fury. 'I tell you, Tanya. This man doesn't deserve our sympathy.'

I can't help but laugh, and soon, my mild giggles turn into loud, irrepressible guffaws. Mummy glares at me, displeased by my failure to be as outraged as her.

'Oh come on, Mummy,' I say as the fits of laughter subside and my jaw begins to ache. 'This is hilarious. Stop acting like this. Let the poor chap live a little.'

'How can you talk like that?' Mummy wails. '*Hai Allah*, my daughter's mind has been corrupted.'

Mummy angrily saunters off to watch TV. Lurch gasps to regain his breath after all the pleading and crying he's done. He covers his ears with his palms and closes his eyes in an attempt to expunge the memory of the incident. He groans softly. But I'm much too entertained to interfere in his sorrow. This matter is between him and Mummy. I'm just here to stir controversy without getting too involved. What do I care if Lurch likes a bit of low grade porn?

I keep his DVD on the counter and return to my room. If I ever get to meet this Razia, I must thank her for such a memorable distraction. I couldn't have dreamt up such rich, mindless comedy had I actually fallen asleep.

8 p.m.

My phone beeps just as I am about to drift off. It's a message from Sonia. But this time, it has nothing to do with her story. The message isn't laced with her characteristic indifference or peppered foul words. Sonia has sent me an apology!

'Thanks for defending Khirad today. I'm sorry I couldn't back you up. I'm also sorry about everything else. It was wrong of me to blame you for Saad and Mopsy's *shaadi*.'

The text comes at a time when I'm too exhausted to speak to anyone. But I find it difficult to ignore Sonia's message. Mummy always tells me that an apology should be accepted at least twenty minutes after it is received as a text. She learnt this trick after suffering through many years of anguish as Mrs Shaukat Farid.

Maybe I should hold on for twenty minutes to come to a decision. I could make Sonia wait a bit, sweat it out maybe.

But finally, going against Mummy's rule, I decide against wasting twenty minutes to massage my ego and reply to her immediately. 'No hard feelings, Sonia.'

A minute later, I snuggle into bed and feel a certain lightness of being, as if I've been acquitted in a murder trial. I send her another text that seems a tad too sentimental to sound like me.

'Old friends shouldn't have to apologize. There's always going to be space in our hearts for each other.'

As sleep descends over me, I'm content that I'm carrying one less burden on my shoulders.

11 p.m.

'Tanya, have you heard from Khirad?' a frantic voice bellows from my phone.

I place a glass of chilled water on my bedside table and adjust my pillow against the bedpost. I am in no hurry to answer the question – especially because it comes from him.

Hours earlier, he had agreed to defame Khirad on her former paramour's orders with such nonchalance. And now, he is pretending to be concerned about her well-being. I tell you, this man is a gift-wrapped package of contradictions.

Hafeez has the ability to despair over the destruction he wreaks. It's one of those formidable, sociopathic traits that would leave others bewildered. But I've become quite immune to it.

'Why do you want to know?' I ask, making my tone sound as curt and distant as possible.

'I ... I...' Hafeez stutters as he justifies his new-found concern for Khirad.

'Wait just a bloody second,' I interrupt him. 'Didn't you put together the story on the Gol TV saga for tomorrow's paper? The one that slams Khirad for doing her job?'

'Tanya,' Hafeez says, as if hearing my name in his husky voice will make me relent. 'I had no choice.'

'No choice? Who the fuck are you? Hassan's *pet*? You can easily walk into my house, kiss me, walk out and never speak to me. But you forget your balls when Hassan asks you to do something? Strange.'

'Tanya, don't change the subject. Where is Khirad? The hospital realized its mistake and the authorities sacked the guard. Hassan won't let us take this update in the story for some reason.'

'Why don't you stand up to your Hassan? What's holding you back?'

'Well, I don't want any confrontation. He's experienced, and wise.'

Clearly, Hafeez has lost his sense of judgement ever since Sonia became his only companion.

'Wise? Since when do you believe that? And by the way, I'm sure the hospital authorities have informed Khirad about their decision. You have no reason to get involved. In fact, you have no reason to call me either.'

I throw the last comment in to get a reaction.

'Yeah, I didn't need to,' he says, sounding dejected.

'So why did you?' I ask in anger.

He stammers for a few seconds and abruptly hangs up. I decide against calling him back.

11.30 p.m.

'Hafeez was right,' Khirad tells me over the phone later. 'They've gotten rid of that ass. I feel so vindicated. As if justice has been served.'

She pauses briefly. 'But I do feel bad for the guard,' she continues. 'He probably has mouths to feed as well.

I'll go retract my complaint. Losing his job is punishment enough.'

Khirad sounds a lot more composed and collected than she was earlier today. My friend sounds like she's had a quick mental makeover in the span of a few hours. 'I'm just glad you're fine,' I tell her. 'But you need to lie low for a bit.'

'*Arre,* why? I'm no fugitive. If the real fugitives don't do it, why should I?'

'True. But I'm worried. I doubt the *Daily Image* will publish anything about the guard's dismissal. Hassan won't let it happen.'

'Nothing to worry about,' Khirad chortles. 'I'll tell Gol TV. They'll definitely do something. You just take care of yourself. And please, please, please, get out of that place as soon as possible. You deserve bigger and better.'

I already realized that I needed bigger and better shortly after I slept with Saad. But Khirad is right. I shouldn't be wasting my precious words at a paper like *Daily Image.* So many careers have taken off because of the voices lent by us subs to our reporters. Imagine the pinnacles we could reach if we became selfish and used our dictionaries and grammatical superpowers for ourselves.

9 October 2016

12 a.m.

Topsy's aversion for the PTI and Bilal's undying devotion to the party is frightening me. I see storms in the future – if not in the drawing room, then in the bedroom.

'It's too much!' Topsy says when I ring her. 'Bilal has gone *lattu*, cannot stop talking about the Panama leaks. Our sex is suffering. The other day, I wanted him to go down on me. He obliged, but when I was about to cum, he said the most abominable thing. Ugh, I just can't repeat it. It was outrageous. Incredibly crude.'

'What did your Lahori boy say?' I laugh as I ask her. 'I hope it's something raunchy at least.'

'No, T. No. He called me Panama. Literally screamed, "Yeah, Panama. Yeah, baby. Come already, my precious verdict. Come to papa."'

I stifle the urge to laugh. 'Frankly, I quite like the idea of political roleplaying.'

'I didn't know you have a kinky side,' Topsy teases me.

'My kinks amount to nothing in comparison to what your boy has to offer,' I chuckle.

'I wish he would quit the party already. But enough about me. How are things?'

As soon as I tell her about Khirad's ordeal and Hafeez and Sonia's attempts to woo me back into their lives, Topsy returns to being her usual sassy self.

'That boy really needs to get in your pants,' Topsy says. 'Give it to him already. As for Khirad, poor thing should have slapped him back. That's how Bilal and I do it.'

Topsy's candour is usually quite scarring. Still, there is often a grain of truth to what she says.

'Speaking of Sonia, I have news for you,' she continues. 'Mopsy is having marital trouble with Tintin.'

'Well, as you sow ... But who is Tintin?'

'We call Saad Tintin,' she laughs. 'It's our pet name for him. And they are having problems in the sack, it seems. Mopsy is deeply upset. I think it might end.'

'Should I let Sonia know that she can have him back soon enough?' I quip.

'Be my guest. I'm just glad my man isn't weird in these matters. And at least he knows how to love a woman.'

'And her friends,' I blurt out the words without realizing their implications. But if I know Topsy well enough, she doesn't take umbrage to such remarks. I can sneak them into any conversation – with the same ease I'd sneak boys home during my college days without Mummy suspecting a thing – and she'll simply overlook their presence.

'Don't be hatin' on him,' Topsy feigns anger. 'He might just be a PTI minister one day.'

'We'll see. If Imran locks down Isloo, topples the Nawaz government and become PM, your boyfriend could totally be his foreign affairs adviser or minister. God knows, we could use one already. I'm sure he knows a thing or two about foreign affairs. Didn't you mention he once had a girlfriend in Abu Dhabi?'

'Ha-ha-ha,' Topsy pauses for breath. 'I just hope Imran comes to his senses. He really needs to stop deceiving these Insafians. All of them think they're on a mission to root out corruption. It seems more like *Mission Impossible 2* than a *House of Cards* episode. Bilal just doesn't understand. He's blinded by passion. It's quite pathetic.'

As long as Bilal is pursuing Panama instead of me, I'm happy. Life could have taken a perilous turn for me had PTI not saved the day. But that doesn't mean I will be daft enough to vote for the party.

'Honestly, Topsy, these Insafians are to blame,' I say curtly. 'They make terrible lovers. If you fight, they are prepared to launch a *dharna* against you. If you show the slightest bit of contrition – or, for that matter, relent on your missteps – they see it as a sign of a larger *tabdeeli*. If you make the mistake of loving them, they think the *tabdeeli* has finally come.'

Topsy hoots with laughter. 'Bilal clearly has more game than the other Insafians,' she replies after her laughing fit subsides. 'He'll stand out as an exception.'

'True, his penchants might help him bring some *tabdeeli* in the right places,' I say. 'I could use a little sexual frankness. It might lend some courage to Hafeez. He seems to be playing this distorted version of hide and seek with me … Anyway, let's drink soon,' I conclude, veering the conversation in a safer direction to stop me from thinking about Hafeez. 'It's been ages.'

'We'll celebrate when you've quit that god-awful job of yours,' Topsy says before she hangs up. 'Deal?'

'Deal.'

Suzi ka Halwa

29 October 2016

1 p.m.

I've realized that there are always going to be inflamed radicals around me, the ones who would rather shoot the messenger than understand the message and figure out if there is any truth in it. I would know. One of them gave birth to me.

These days, Mummy has begun to find sadistic pleasure in watching those loud, angry talk shows. Right now, she's obsessed with Cyril Almeida's front-page story on a confrontation between civilian leaders and the military.

When I come downstairs and plonk myself on the sofa, she's at it again. I scoff and rummage for the remote. 'You know, just because your Indian soap operas aren't being aired anymore doesn't mean you have the licence to watch such nonsense,' I say to her.

'*Chup karo*,' she hisses. 'This is a very important show. Your Aunty Saira was telling me about it.'

148

I've never been a fan of political whodunits. But I'm not indifferent to the Cyril debacle. For little over two weeks, a group of analysts have been seen on talk shows, wagging their razor-sharp tongues against Cyril like a motley crew of judgemental mothers-in-law. Poor Cyril has seen enough peril and deserves to be left alone already. I can't even imagine what he went through when he was placed on the no-fly list. If I were in his place, I don't know what I'd do to get permission to travel again.

Now, I look at her and say with scathing firmness, 'You should stick to your Star Plus serials. Politics is not for the frivolous.'

Though she is a PTI enthusiast, Mummy has always had an aversion to radical movements. Every five years, she prays for the man on the hot seat – she never liked Benazir because Daddy had a crush on her – as if he is the sole provider of roti, *kapda* and (in Mummy's case) *kapde ki dukaan* (she already has a *makaan*, you see).

'You're one to talk, *beta*,' Mummy's tone is peppered with smug confidence and sarcasm. 'I'm not the one who is going to interview a *halwai*. Some serious journalist you are.'

'Mummy,' I prop my hands on my hips. 'When you make such remarks about my career, I always feel the need to remind you that you are the sole reason why I am not a full-time reporter.'

She only laughs, clapping her hands like a monkey.

I scowl at her. But she continues to giggle to herself. Thankfully, her laughter or even the sting of her words isn't poisonous to me anymore. Over time, the snide, snarky nature of our conversations has begun to slide off me. But in Mummy's defence, I am actually going to interview the owner of a sweetshop – though not one of those conventional *ones* who have been in the business for years and want to shield their centuries-old secret recipe from the devious clutches of jealous competitors. This one finds consolation in age-old customs that she – yes, this *halwai* is a woman – has managed to appropriate, repackage and sell at exorbitant prices. She is called Suzi, she belongs to the privileged elite and has a fetish for all things 'local'. The fact that her confectionery business – which is fittingly called Suzi *ka* Halwa – attracts a premium, proves that people in this city are stupid enough to buy anything.

'*Khair*, Suzi isn't just a bored housewife with grand ambitions,' I say defensively. 'She's a businesswoman and blogger who thrives on destroying the reputation of new restaurants in the city.'

'*Achcha*,' Mummy coos. 'And how does this make it any better?'

'Today is my golden opportunity to get back at her for all the catty remarks she made about the hygiene practices of some roadside establishments which were then forced to close down. So you see, what I'm doing serves the national interest as well.'

'The aren't real battles, *beta*,' Mummy says, adjusting herself on the sofa.

'At least *halwai*s have something sweet to offer, Mummy,' I reply, my voice soaked in sarcasm. 'Which is more than what I can say for you.'

After firing that last shot, I walk out the main door. Mummy returns to watching her talk show as the door latch clicks into place.

2 p.m.

Suzi *ka* Halwa is nothing like Willy Wonka's chocolate factory. Much to my dismay, it's a boxlike shop on Khayaban-e-Ittehad with a tacky green neon sign and black, marble-encrusted walls. Its imperfections become all the more visible when I enter it.

The least Suzi could have done was cough up some dough to do up the interiors. The inside is as tacky as the outside, and for someone with the snark Suzi displays about other outlets' shortcomings, I'd expected better.

Fifteen minutes into my interview with Suzi, the burning temptation to ask her a million questions leaves me restless and impatient. But Suzi, as I begin to realize during the course of the interview, has a way of evading questions she cannot answer. She calls it 'people skills'.

'And this is my Lindt chocolate halwa,' Suzi points towards a silver tray inside a glass cabinet. 'Who needs *kishmish* with their halwa when you have chocolate sprinkles? It's a favourite among my customers.'

Now I don't mean to be unfair here, but I wince at concepts like gulab jamuns dipped in Hershey's syrup. It's not as though I think there should be rules against this. I firmly believe that all boundaries need to be porous – but this halwa joint is plain ridiculous. It's astonishing to see the bizarre things people do to appear innovative.

'So tell me, Suzi,' I say. 'What is your clientele like? And where do you see the business going?'

I'm beginning to feel annoyed with myself. Mummy is right. I don't need to interview such people to be recognized as a journalist.

'Well, umm ...' Suzi stammers. 'I have a supportive group of friends who have helped me set up the business and will help me take it to new heights.'

'Is that so?' I ask, propelled by the sudden desire to be bitchy.

'Yes ... you know, Bina Hassan,' she whispers. 'She has contributed a large chunk of her soon-to-be ex-husband's wealth to my shop. She's a true friend.'

I wonder if Suzi will have any regrets about blurting out these details in my presence once the interview is over. After all, Bina is Hassan's soon to be ex-wife. And Hassan isn't the sort to forgive such transgressions. I can imagine him fretting over the double-column slot Suzi *ka* Halwa will get in tomorrow's paper. He'd loathe me for writing a profile about the woman who has unjustly inherited his wealth and spent it on a fancy halwa shop.

2.35 p.m.

'Tanya, darling,' Suzi says as I prepare to leave. 'Don't forget to take your Lindt chocolate halwa for the road.'

Does she expect me to actually eat all that garbage? Maybe I'll try it out on Mummy instead.

'Sure thing,' I say, struggling to appear as impassive as I can. 'I'll take it for my city editor, Hassan.'

A broad smile floods Suzi's face, as if what I said was an affirmation of her many achievements in the confectionery business. She doesn't have the intellect to understand that I'm giving her a friendly reminder about her faux pas. All her *hard work* in opening this joint could be easily ruined by the hammer strokes of Hassan's editorial judgement.

'Yes, do give Hassan my love,' she coos and then winks at me. I don't know what to make of this gesture.

She must be dumber than I had understood her to be.

Still, my instinct tells me that the matter is far more complex. Why would Bina give Hassan's hard-earned money – that is, if you call flirting with idioms, young female reporters and NGO officials hard work – to Suzi? Has Hassan also slept with Suzi in the past? That could explain why she winked at me. But if Suzi was one of the many other women, did Bina give her the money to spite Hassan?

I wonder how I can figure out this complicated web of possible theories. Where's Mummy when I actually need her? Gossip isn't everyone's cup of tea. And Mummy's brew is a lot stronger because she has direct access to the concerned party. She would be able to get all the answers directly from Bina Hassan.

At this point, though, I just need to file this story and squeeze it on to tomorrow's pages without Hassan realizing that it has been published.

But honestly, Hassan is hardly interested in the paper beyond his own NGO plugs. I doubt he'll notice anything.

3 p.m.

'*Yaar*, do you really think you should run the profile on Suzi?' Khirad's concern filters through the telephone. Her question fills me with anger. Is she really even trying to defend Hassan?

When my Captain peeps at me through their rearview mirror, I register the fear in his eyes as he catches sight of my scowling face.

'What do you mean?' I ask Khirad in astonishment. 'I have to publish it. And why shouldn't I? Because Suzi is Hassan's estranged wife's friend? That's no reason!'

Khirad senses my impatience and skilfully lowers her voice.

'Let's not trouble him any further, babe,' she whispers. 'I don't want you getting into trouble. As it is, he knows you were partly responsible for the condoms episode. I didn't tell him anything. He said some peon at the office heard you talking to me.'

Is Khirad dumb enough to really believe that?

'Khirad,' I try to speak patiently and slowly. 'How could a peon who barely understands a word of English overhear me telling you to send a packet of condoms to Hassan's house?'

'Then how could Hassan find out? Oh! Do you think he spied on us that day?' Khirad sounds scared.

'He does have a paranoid streak,' I say. 'But I doubt he'd go as far as spying on people.'

Khirad doesn't say anything, but I can feel her worry through the phone.

'I still don't care what he says about the story,' I revert to the original topic, the anger rising within me once again like molten lead. 'The *Daily Image* isn't Hassan's personal property.'

'Tanya,' I detect a hint of impatience in Khirad's tone. 'I just want you to be safe. Hassan isn't exactly the sanest boss you can have. And honestly, do you think he won't make life difficult for you if you go after him like this? He's anyway been having a hard time.'

Wait, was that a smidgen of sympathy for Hassan? Is Khirad out of her bloody mind?

'Look at you, defending your former lover. Do I hear wedding bells?'

Khirad laughs like a shrill hyena. '*Nahi yaar*, I'm over him, especially after all the bitching and backbiting. I just feel like he's suffered already. Why put him through more?'

If Sonia had said something like this, I would have immediately disregarded her views. But Khirad, I have come to realize, doesn't act without weighing out all the alternatives. I can see that there is some sense in what she's saying, and anyway, it's not like Suzi's profile is going to win me the Pulitzer.

'All right, I won't submit the story.'

'I'm glad,' Khirad says, and after exchanging byes, we hang up.

As the car turns into the office lane, I tell myself that it doesn't matter if I've lost the opportunity to get a byline on a silly story like Suzi's halwa shop. I want to do stories that matter.

Mummy is right. I'm not a serious journalist. If I want to become a good journalist, I'll need to explore the social fabric of my time, peel away its layers until I become familiar with what lies beneath its smooth surface.

Okay, that's just a bit too intense. I need a smoke. And maybe a drink.

4 p.m.

'Tanya Bibi,' Hassan says as he walks into the newsroom. 'Can I see you in my office?'

'Sure,' I nod, staring at my computer to avoid his eyes. 'Let me get done with editing Sonia's story first.'

He struts off to his room and I turn towards Sonia.

'This is a good story,' I smile. 'To be honest, editing your stories has become a lot less difficult lately. You've been putting in a lot more effort to make your copy stronger.'

'A broken relationship does that to you,' Sonia responds glumly. 'The moment someone walks out of your life, you begin to reflect on your own faults. With time, you come up with an elaborate plan to change the course of your life and – if you're lucky – you succeed.'

'Self-pity won't help you, Sonia,' I cock my head against my shoulder. 'What you need to do is move on.'

She rubs her eyes and mops her cheeks with a tissue.

'If you ask me, I'd rather lock myself in a room after a breakup and eat OPTP crisps while watching *Gilmore Girls*,' I tell her in an attempt to make her laugh. 'Who cares if I get fat and the *rishta* aunties reject me like I'm tainted merchandise?'

'Tanya Bibi,' Hassan returns to my desk, having placed his briefcase – yes, he carries one to work – in his office and returned to the newsroom. 'It's urgent.'

'Okay. I'll be there soon,' I tell him and he leaves once more.

'Oh God, now what did I do?' I say as soon as he's out of earshot.

Sonia chortles. 'Maybe you forgot to throw in an idiom in that zoo story from last week,' she suggests, smiling from ear to ear.

'Or it's something a lot more sinister.'

Whatever it is, it can't be that bad. After. all, I've decided against writing that story on Suzi *ka* Halwa because I don't want his ego to be hurt by me. Not many people do that for their boss – especially a loathsome one like Hassan. He owes me a raise and a new idea with which I can earn a byline.

4.10 p.m.

'What's the matter?' I ask as I enter Hassan's office.

Hassan rises from his seat and walks over to his bookshelf.

The shelves used to be empty because Hassan's idea of good journalism has nothing to do with reading. But over the past few months, we subeditors and reporters have been donating books to him, in the hope that he learns a thing or two from them. Hassan now has a bookshelf that is crammed with the works of all the best writers that he has never read – Dostoevsky, Tagore, Manto, Sethu and Jamsheed Marker. It's quite an eclectic collection. But Hassan has never touched a single book after it has been placed on the shelf. When a book is donated to him, Hassan inspects it with the severity of a security guard at a high-risk airport. I suspect that he thought we were gifting him bombs in the form of books.

Seeing Hassan pacing in front of the bookshelf, I am gripped by the desire to giggle. But he appears to be in a foul mood.

'I have a question to ask you, Tanya Bibi. And I expect an honest reply.'

'Sure,' I say. All the hilarity I felt just a moment ago disappears. The atmosphere has become tense and I'm pulled in by the seriousness of his tone. My heart races with fevered misery.

'Have I done anything to harm you? Or, let me put it this way – do you despise me for some reason?'

What a question? Do I hate him? I feel like giggling again. *'How do I hate you? Let me count the ways. I hate how you led Khirad on and tried to take advantage of her. I hate those blasted idioms with which I have to clutter sentences just because of you. I hate how you can make non-stories seem important because some contact at an NGO pays you a hefty sum to do so.'*

Of course, these thoughts are exclusively private. But oh, how I wish I could at least say one of these things to his face.

'Tanya Bibi, what's the matter? Why are you silent?'

'I don't exactly understand what you are trying to say, sir,' I respond diplomatically, staring into his big, beady eyes.

A twisted smile appears on his face. 'Sir? Now you call me sir?' his voice rises in anger. 'Well, I was also your sir when Khirad sent a packet of condoms to my house after you told her to. I was also your sir when you went and interviewed that no-good Sabeena's halwa store.'

For a second, I'm distracted. How is Suzi short for Sabeena? This is truly the height of pretentiousness.

'Sabeena called me a while ago and told me that you were at her halwa store,' he continues. 'She wanted to thank me for sending a journalist over. She thought it was a goodwill gesture considering that useless wife of mine gave her a large chunk of *my* money.'

I was right about Suzi. She truly is the embodiment of stupidity. I can imagine how the telephone conversation must have gone. And now she's put me in this mess.

'Well, I was planning to do the story because I thought it would be interesting to see a female *halwai* modernize traditional halwa on a retail level,' I struggle to curb the rebellion in my voice in case I begin to sound defensive. 'But when I realized who Suzi was, I decided against doing the story because it didn't seem right.'

'Oh, how generous of you.'

Hassan lights a cigarette. He returns to his seat and plonks himself on the chair.

'You know, I've met a few women like you at this office,' his tone grows deliberately soft, as if he is disclosing a secret. 'I appreciate all the work you do. You're a good sub and an excellent writer.'

'Thank you, sir,' I say, knowing perfectly well that he is only massaging my ego and will gradually lure me into the dark, mysterious core of what he actually wants to say.

'You're also an excellent liar,' he says menacingly. He takes a generous puff of his cigarette and blows grey rings into the air.

'Sorry, sir?'

'You've been lying about your feelings all along,' he says. He winks and moves his hand closer to me. 'You told Khirad to send me the condoms because you wanted things to end between me and her. You decided to interview Sabeena because you wanted scoops on my

married life. I think it's obvious that you have feelings
for me, Tanya Bibi. You're acting out because of those
feelings. But now that I'm free, I don't mind taking things
forward.'

Men can be so damn presumptuous. I always
thought Saad was the one who needed a tight slap for
assuming that every woman in the world wanted him.
But Hassan is part of a different breed of egotistical
sleazeballs altogether.

'Hassan, you're way off the mark,' my voice is
confident once again. I don't need to be scared of this
asshole. 'I love how you assume women act against each
other. I did everything that you've accused me of because
Khirad is my friend. As for Suzi's interview, it was a mere
coincidence.'

'Don't lie, Tanya Bibi,' he insists. 'I know women.'

'I'm sure you do,' I say, making every attempt to sound
sardonic. 'But then you must also know that I'm quite
done with you, your attitude and your twisted brand of
journalism.'

There you go. I've said it. And it didn't even take
too much emotional energy. Topsy owes me booze.
Tanya Shaukat has finally decided to quit her job. Why?
Well, I know I've taken this decision on a whim. But
a conceited man like Hassan shouldn't be allowed to
bully me into an awkward position like this. I'd rather
walk out of this ugly marriage of convenience on my
own terms.

Hassan laughs and then fidgets with his pen.

'Where will you go? Which newspaper will take you?
The *Daily Image* created you. You are because we are.

You'll never be able to survive. Look at what's happening to journalists across the world. Actually, forget the world. Think about your own country. Look at what's happening to Cyril.'

'Well, Hassan,' I adjust my seat closer to his desk and rest my hands on it. 'Cyril has an advantage.'

Hassan stares pensively at me. No journalist can support the idea of imposing restrictions on the media. But I've noticed that when it comes to Cyril, Hassan's principles often falter or eventually crumble without fail. After all, Cyril works for our competitors and deserves not even a shred of sympathy and goodwill.

'Dare I ask what this advantage is?' Hassan sounds facetious, as if he expects a silly response that will leave him giggling for days at a stretch.

'He has the support of his editor,' I say, without mincing my words. 'Unlike you, his editor is willing to stand by him. I doubt you'd have the courage to take such a step.'

I have to admit that this was possibly the bravest – and, arguably, the cruelest – thing I could have said to Hassan. But as they say, you should never withhold something that rightfully belongs to someone else. It is Hassan's right to hear this jibe from me. It's an added bonus if he finds it harsh. There is, at least, an iota of truth to what I've said. He might as well get used to hearing such things. Who knows, it might even benefit him.

'Leave,' Hassan says with a brusqueness that stings me. 'Just get out. Once and for all. Take all your things and leave.'

I can hear excited whispers emanating from the cubicles outside Hassan's room. A group of reporters appear to have gathered outside the office to watch me confront a man whom they loathe in equal measure. I can hear Sonia talking frantically to them. Is Hafeez worried too?

'Don't labour under the illusion that you've fired me, Hassan. As I told you earlier, I quit.'

I storm out of the room, rush towards my desk and grab my bag. Sonia holds out her hand and places it on my shoulder as everyone else stares at me – as if I'm re-enacting an emotional scene from *Humsafar*. Hafeez isn't in the room. I blink back the tears from flowing through my eyelashes – I wouldn't want to ruin my makeup – push aside Sonia's hand and rummage through my drawers to collect my belongings. I gather a map of Karachi, which I'd pinned on the board above my desk, a guidebook on editing and an old lighter that Hafeez and I once used.

I spot the box of Lindt chocolate halwa lying next to my computer. Now what do I with this? Suzi's halwa has cost me a job. But it also helped me summon the strength to confront Hassan.

'Tanya, listen,' Sonia says, holding out her palm again. She's visibly startled by the way the situation has escalated. I continue clearing my desk and ignore her.

I don't want to listen. The desire to listen – or even to be heard – has been obliterated. I just want to get out of here.

As I prepare to leave, the box of halwa looms like a spectre in my troubled mind. Its tormenting presence threatens to assail me. So far, my exit from the office seems to be a bit too banal. I could use something to perk things up and this halwa box is probably the best lethal weapon of choice. Intuitively, I strut back into Hassan's office with the box.

'This is for you,' I say, placing the box on his desk, next to the book on idioms and a packet of ORS. 'It's a pile of shit. But guess what, it has been produced using your own money. Enjoy.'

I walk out of Hassan's office and zip past the gossiping reporters and a weeping Sonia – I guess there won't be a water shortage in the *basti* today – and make my way out of the building.

The thoughts that stream through my mind as I book a Careem and make my way home have little to do with my newfound status as an unemployed journalist. They are about Hafeez. Together, we smoked, laughed, argued about politics and ate desi Chinese food for the many long hours that we spent at this hellhole. It was in the newsroom that I first caught a glimpse of Hafeez's views and began secretly admiring them. Over the years, the office had become the embodiment of our silent struggle to overcome work pressure and balance it with the hunger to live. And lately – thanks to Sonia and Inder – it had become the site of our silent exchanges and the breeding ground of conflicts. Even our unsaid goodbyes could not provide us closure. As I walk out, I know Hafeez won't be out of my life. He'll crawl back in like a lead actor in Mummy's Indian soap operas. Though I do hope that he can at least dress better.

6 p.m.

Mummy's reaction to my quitting the *Daily Image* is abysmal – just as I had expected.

'*Beta,* this is an extreme reaction,' my mother says as she watches a Pakistani drama on Hum TV. She seems to have graduated from talk shows at a quick pace. Did Mummy fight with Aunty Saira while I was making key decisions in life? Or has she finally understood how silly those talk shows are?

'The man tried to get me to sleep with him,' I respond sharply. 'I'm sure my reaction was justified.'

'*Beta*, you're too young for principles.' Mummy appears unfazed by what I've told her. 'You should never leave a decent job. What are you going to do now? Should I start looking for boys?'

'Mummy, calm down, will you?' I say. 'I'll be fine. I have some cash to last me a while. There are some freelance opportunities that I can avail as well.'

From the nervous way in which Mummy is looking at me, it appears she is unconvinced by my explanation. That's the problem with having a mother who lacks the empathy and courage to take a stand. Now if I were Shabana Azmi or Benazir Bhutto's daughter, things would be different.

'I'll call Mimi or Saira,' Mummy mumbles and walks to the phone in the lounge. 'It's time to intervene.'

Great. Another round of *rishta*-shopping is about to begin. I should stay as far away from home as I can. If I don't, I'll find myself trapped on yet another string of dates with Ahmar the boring businessman or Sohaib the mama-loving nut job who, had insisted that we share a room with his widowed mother after marriage. I can't afford to take such risks. Nothing can be allowed to impinge on my freedom. It has to go through me first.

'Mummy,' I walk over to the phone and yank the receiver out of her hands. 'Why can't you back off a little? Why must you poke your nose in all my affairs? This is my decision. Accept it and back off. No one is asking for your consent. Or Mimi's or Saira's input, for that matter.'

Mummy's face turns ashen at my outburst. I feel strangely relieved, even rejuvenated by my sudden display of uninhibited rage towards her. Even though my telling her off was fuelled by an impulse, it was the culmination of my anger and frustration with her meddlesome ways. After a long time, a burden seems to have been miraculously lifted from the inner chambers of my heart and unleashed directly against the person responsible.

'Fine,' Mummy's voice cracks. 'I was just looking out for your best interests. *Khair*, what can a mother do when her own child considers her to be a stranger?'

With theatrical restraint, Mummy rubs her eyes with her dupatta and hobbles back to the sofa in front of the TV. Why is she such a drama queen?

'Haji, *bring me my chai!*' she hollers. By the way she's now ignoring me, I can tell she's putting on a show for the alleged pain and pressure she's feeling after being spurned by her own daughter.

Lurch scurries out of the kitchen with a cup of steaming chai within minutes.

'Begum Sahib, *and pakore*?' he asks.

She waves her hand to shoo Lurch away and he
shuffles back into the kitchen. *Hai*, they'd make such a
cute couple if one of them wasn't such an imbecile and
the other wasn't such a drama queen.

If I know my mother well enough, she will vent her
anger by eating a lot of food over the next few hours
and we'll be on speaking terms again by tomorrow.
Mummy always finds a way to make herself the centre
of attention. Unfortunately for her, she has a daughter
with similar tendencies.

6.30 p.m.

Khirad's reaction wasn't what I had expected it to be.

'I warned you, Tanya,' she hollers into the phone. 'I
told you not to anger him. That man is lethal.'

'Let it be,' I tell her. 'Lethal *hoga apne ghar pe*. If he
tries to jump out of his pants, I'll make sure something
gets stuck in his zipper.'

'That's all well and good. But what are you going to
do now? Why don't you come to Gol TV?'

'I'd rather die of natural causes than endure the ordeal
of being slapped by a security guard on live television,' I
laugh. 'I'll figure it out. For now, I just want to celebrate
my independence.'

'You can enjoy your independence,' Khirad says,
pulling me out of my reverie. 'But you'll need to find a
new job soon.'

Even though I'm the one out of a job, Khirad is the one
sounding more anxious. I think she fears that the shame of
losing my job will affect me sooner than later.

'I'm not sure if I want to find a new job,' I respond hesitatingly. 'There's so much more to explore at this point. I've wasted away working as a sub. I think it's time to do something that interests me, enhances my creative abilities.'

'Do you have a concrete plan in mind?' she asks. She doesn't sound patronizing or cruel, just genuinely compassionate.

'Maybe or maybe not,' I yawn, deliberately evading her question.

Khirad clicks her tongue. Her disapproval of the choices I have made on a whim makes me acutely aware of the difference between us. This new situation doesn't rankle me. But even in her concern, Khirad is not being malicious or condescending.

'Just make sure you know what you're doing,' Khirad tells me in earnest. 'I wouldn't want you to suffer like I did.'

'What do you mean?' I ask her, curious.

'In the 1990s, my father used to run a small Urdu newspaper in Karachi,' Khirad begins after letting out a long sigh. 'He was heavily critical of the MQM and was shot dead in Azizabad.'

'Oh god, that's dreadful,' I gasp. 'How old were you?'

'I was only five years old,' Khirad's voice is tearful now.

'Did you ever find out who was behind the killing?'

'That's a naïve question,' she replies. 'All of us know who killed him. But the matter was never reported properly and was eventually forgotten.'

'Do you miss him?' I ask her, the memories of the invisible wounds left by Daddy's intermittent presence during my college years returning to me.

'Unbearably,' she whispers. 'My mother worked hard to ensure that we completed our education. When she fell ill, I had to get a job to support her.'

'Did your mother approve of your decision to become a journalist?'

'She didn't. But I couldn't stay away. I had to honour my father's memory.'

'You're very brave,' I say. 'You're far more courageous than me or anyone else.'

'Brave women don't fool around with their bosses,' she giggles.

'To be fair, that was just a mistake,' I say. 'As it is, he is a vile man who had no qualms about defaming you. And you showed him that no one could mess with you and get away with it.'

'Tanya,' she pauses for breath. 'Thanks for being a pillar of support. I'll let you know if I hear of any job opportunities for you.'

As I cut the call, Khirad's words cling to my mind. How can I write a piece for Inder about people's perceptions of violence in Kashmir when I'm trapped in my ivory tower – where not even a murmur of what lies outside can be heard?

7 p.m.

'We must celebrate, darling,' Topsy's inebriated voice booms through the receiver. 'Finally. How did your little friends react to it? Did Hafeez cry you a river?'

'Are you kidding me? He wasn't even there when I left. Fuck knows what he was up to at that point.'

'Screw him, he's a forgotten chapter. Let's celebrate tonight. My place.'

'Sure thing. I'll call Adam as well. He knows how to party in style.'

'Definitely. I'll tell Bilal to wear some pants.'

'Ah, an early start in the bedroom today?'

'I wish,' Topsy says with a twinge of disappointment. 'He's left PTI.'

'What? Before the *dharna*?' I say, alarmed. 'Didn't he just join the party? What happened?'

'He realized that he was chasing youthful idealism,' Topsy appears to have rote-learnt the answer. 'Also, I refused to have sex with him until he called it quits.'

I pause for a second, plug my headphones into my cell phone and check my messages. Sonia has called thrice and left fourteen messages since I last saw her. Her concern appears to be genuine enough. But I'm in no mood for a sappy conversation about what happened. I just want to distract myself a little and drown my miseries in booze. Quitting your job can be a heady experience and carousing helps erase the internal politics and friction from your memory. It's an important rite of passage.

'That's what happens to our revolutionaries in this day,' Topsy continues. 'You scare them with the possibility of a dry spell in the bedroom and they come crawling back.'

'I'm impressed,' I say as I distractedly read through Sonia's silly and sentimental messages about how much she will miss me. 'I've never doubted your prowess. But now, I respect it even more.'

'Ha-ha, but that's not the only reason,' Topsy replies. 'Everyone expects a soft coup in the country and Bilal's mother is insecure about what might happen. She told him to quit and he listened.'

'I never expected Bilal, of all people, to be a mama's boy,' I say, surprised.

'Most of them are, darling,' Topsy clicks her tongue. 'Anyway, I'll see you soon.'

The moment she cuts the call, I put my phone away. I pluck out a cigarette from an old packet of Marlboro Lights that I found near my dresser and forage through my bag for the lighter I brought home from work. To my surprise, it still has some fluid in it. I light up. There's no better way to end an irksome day than with a cigarette. Now that I'm jobless, I should consider taking a hiatus from the past and adopt a new avatar – a fresh skin that I can flaunt with renewed confidence.

The Kaptaan Chappal

29 October 2016

9 p.m.

Bilal isn't the only one who has to sustain the pressures of a dry spell. Ever since the high court decided to revoke the licences of wine shops in Sindh, the desert province has become all the more dry, arid and unbearable. Everyone I know is searching for a foolproof strategy to climb out of this predicament.

Narendra, my trusted bootlegger, also seems to be on edge lately. The court's decision is a double-edged sword – a *churi* with a *benefit*. On the one hand, he fears getting caught with all his wares and being accused of spreading the corrupting influences of the West and, on the other, he is delighted at the prospect of charging high prices for his valuable commodities. Trust Narendra to be so cunning, so unabashedly self-serving. Every time I call Narendra to restock my supplies, he finds a way to aggravate me.

'So much money for a bottle of Absolut?!' I find myself yelling at him over the phone.

'Take it or leave it,' he says with an air of condescension. The high court has created a monster who is drunk on power and high on sass. I could just wring his neck. But I don't want to suffer through a dry spell – not tonight at least.

'What else do you have?' I ask, struggling to remain composed.

'I have raspberry Smirnoff. Very cheap.'

It does sound absurdly cheap. How will I get a buzz with the sour tang of raspberries on my tongue? I'm not some teenager that Narendra can fool into buying something nobody wants.

'What's that?' I ask sternly. 'I've never heard of this.'

'Get with the times, everyone is drinking it these days.' There is a peculiar smugness to Narendra's tone that makes me want to slaughter him like a goat. God, I wish it were Bakri Eid.

I'm the one who moves with the times. In fact, the movers and shakers turn to me for instructions before they decide to set trends. Narendra needs to stop acting like his namesake. The world can only handle one of them at a time.

'*Theek hai, theek hai,* I'll take that.'

Once the court lifts the ban – such pious bans only last a few days – I'll make it a point to get back at Narendra for this. And you won't even need another round of elections to see that day.

9.45 p.m.

Bootlegger runs in Karachi are replete with the thrill of adventure and the crippling fear of getting caught. But when you're with Adam, the experience has a distinct kind of pleasure.

As we drive down to Khayaban-e-Shahbaz to collect our booze, Adam updates me about his romantic sexcapades. Meeting him always gives me unbridled joy – the kind Sonia saps from me with her mere presence. There is never a shortage of stories and gossip that we can share between shots of vodka. I don't recall there ever being a single spell of silence between us whenever we have hung out.

'I completely forgot to tell you,' Adam says, as he steers his red Suzuki past Sultan Masjid. 'Mohib and Ibrahim are together now.'

'Wait, what? How did that happen?'

'It's so surreal,' he says with a mournful look on his face. 'I didn't know how to react.'

'I understand that coupling can be a mysterious pursuit,' I say. 'But this is plain ridiculous. Love triangles aren't meant to be *so* complicated.'

Adam always manages to outdo me in these matters. He seems to attract more drama than I do, but to his credit, he has the stamina to tackle it with aplomb.

'Well, it all began when I decided to pursue the weird connection I had with Mohib,' Adam lets out a breath. 'He used to take out time from his *marsiya*s and biting expeditions and we'd go for long drives and chai.'

Long drives and chai? How dreadfully unromantic! I hope this is a euphemism for some juicier details.

'It was all going well until a week ago,' Adam continues as I try to fill in the blanks on what happened between the long drives and chai. 'I made the mistake of taking him to a party to which Ibrahim was also invited. The moment he saw Mohib and I walk in, Ibrahim started hovering around us like a bloody *makkhi*. Within a matter of minutes, he had bitten my date and Mohib had bitten him back. By the end of the night, Mohib dumped me for Ibrahim.'

'I've always been fascinated by men who think they have what it takes to be a Casanova,' I say sarcastically.

'You can say that again,' Adam laughs. 'They parade around the city, spreading mischief like it's a form of charity.'

'But this Ibrahim of yours thinks he's some Greek God. Even Aristotle Onassis was grounded in some ways. I can't imagine Ibrahim standing outside your window, pleading for forgiveness.'

'I'm not Maria Callas, sadly.' A smirk conceals Adam's disappointment.

'Still, his behaviour is just vile,' I say, feeling defensive of my friend. 'Didn't you confront Ibrahim or Mohib about this? What did they say?'

'That *chutia* Ibrahim said he did it for my benefit,' Adam breaks a traffic light and the policeman standing there throws him a death stare. 'He said Mohib wasn't good for me. So he figured that before I decided to hog him for myself, he should come with an elaborate ruse to keep us apart.'

Ibrahim's logic reminds me of the good old days when I'd sleep with Sonia's love interests and tell her that they weren't worth it. Of course, Sonia's case is different from Adam's because he isn't naïve like her. Whenever Sonia liked someone, her limited brain cells and every artery that ran through to her heart would conspire to read her *nikah* with the guy and delude her into dreaming about a prosperous marriage with a man whom she had barely spoken to. Adam isn't the sort to have mind babies with men. He just wants to be happy – even if he can be a tad frightening.

'Wasn't Ibrahim getting married?' I ask, suddenly remembering that the Casanova's ego was set to be deflated by a henpecked bride of his family's choosing.

'He wants both. A man and a wife. He basically wants Mohib and me along with that fiancée of his.'

'Together?' I ask, instinctively moving my hand to cover my mouth. 'Or *alag alag?*'

'Don't be silly,' Adam says. His smile fades and a stern expression appears on his face. 'He wants the best of both worlds. A wife who'll cook and give him bouncing baby boys and a man who'll be his boy-toy.'

'All it takes is one kick to put such people on the right track.' I clench my fist with fury. 'The question is, will you be able to kick him in the right places?'

'I want nothing to do with that man,' Adam says, wiping a lone teardrop that has travelled down to his cheekbone. 'He's gone too far this time.'

10.15 p.m.

'Narendra never comes on time,' I complain to Adam.

'How do you know when he comes?' he asks, giggling at his own juvenile humour.

'Don't be silly,' I bite out in impatience. 'I'm not talking about what you think I'm talking about. I don't fantasize about bootleggers. I fantasize about their wares.'

Adam switches on the radio and croons to an old Nazia Hassan song.

'We've been waiting under a neem tree on a dark street for close to twenty minutes,' I complain. 'We could get mugged. But why should he care?'

'In the black market customers can't always be right, T,' Adam says. He switches off the radio as the song comes to an end. 'The balance always tilts in the supplier's favour, as if he is god and we're the small things that bow down to him.'

I run a finger through my hair as I keep an eye on the road.

'I know I have no reason to complain because good things always come to those who wait. But this is just outrageous. He should be more punctual.'

'Especially with the police on alert because of the closure of wine shops,' Adam interjects, reminding me that we could get into trouble with the cops tonight.

'Exactly,' I grumble.

'Chill, he'll be here soon,' Adam says, even though he knows perfectly well that we could be waiting for a long time.

10.20 p.m.

There is a knock on the car window.

'Thank god, he's here,' Adam says, rolling down the window. 'I thought he'd...'

Adam falls silent mid-sentence. I turn to face him and then look out the window. I didn't know Narendra had cropped his wavy black tresses – they used to fall down to his shoulders – and that he has started wearing Armani suits. I'm sure it adds legitimacy to his clandestine craft and draws in good business.

'Oh for fuck's sake,' Adam fumes. 'Ibrahim, what the fuck are you doing here? Have you been following me?' *Oh*.

I've been hearing about Ibrahim for months. But I never realized how dapper Adam's Casanova was until now. Storytelling is an art and, like most of my friends, Adam never fails to disappoint me with his scattered, patchy narratives.

Ibrahim pulls open the door, hops into the back seat and holds out his hand for me to shake.

'Hi, I'm Ibrahim,' he says in an impeccable baritone voice. 'You must be Tanya. I've heard a lot about you.'

'I've heard a lot about you too,' I say snidely.

Ibrahim winks at me. 'I'm guessing you'll be joining us tonight as well?'

'No, thanks,' I respond coldly, bowing my head to prevent myself from falling for his good looks. 'I'm not into that kind of stuff. Now that I've seen you, I doubt it would work.'

'Oh, that can be arranged,' Ibrahim snorts as he giggles.

'Cut we could *make* it work,' Adam admonishes his ex-boyfriend. 'What do you want? Why are you following me?'

'I want you, *meri jaan*,' Ibrahim grabs Adam's hand and holds it against his chest. 'Mohib was a passing fancy. I couldn't imagine life without you. I've left him. I just want you.'

'But you're getting married,' Adam says. He pats Ibrahim's shoulder and pushes him towards the car door. 'And you also wanted time.'

'I've taken time and have reached a decision,' Ibrahim says with robotic sternness.

He pauses for oxygen and then falls silent, as if waiting for a reaction from us. Adam and I stare intently at Ibrahim, eager to hear his final verdict on the fate of their relationship. If I were Adam, I'd slap him for taking such a crucial decision in such an insensitive manner.

'I've decided to marry and still be with you on the side.'

Adam presses his hands against the steering wheel and looks towards the dusty windshield.

'And what makes you think I'll agree to this?' Adam speaks through his teeth.

'Your undying love for me, baby.' Ibrahim leans against the back seat, leaving shoe stains on the upholstery. '*Aur nahi toh kya?*'

For someone who is trying to win back his estranged lover, Ibrahim is rather cocky. I wish I could have the honour of putting him in his place. All I will need is one of my stilettos.

But Adam divests me of this glorious pleasure just as I think about it. He yanks off his sturdy Kaptaan chappal and flings it at Ibrahim. Forgetting his smugness, the Armani-clad Ibrahim ducks his head and holds up his hands to shield his face. Adam throws his other chappal at his ex-boyfriend. Now *that's* how you deal with men like Ibrahim. I admit that this whole situation reminds me of what Sonia did to me the night that she was jilted. But I don't feel even a smidgen of sympathy for Ibrahim. Not all victims are innocent, you see.

'Get out! Get the fuck out, Ibrahim!'

Ibrahim hurriedly unlocks the door and makes a run for it. Immediately, Adam opens the front door, grabs his chappal and gets out of the car.

In the distance, I can see Narendra exiting his white Corolla. Ibrahim runs in the same direction, with his shirt sticking out of his black trousers and his dishevelled hair glistening under a lone streetlight. Possessed with rage, Adam flings his chappal at Ibrahim. The Kaptaan chappal – like the Kaptaan himself – misses its target and instead hits Narendra's belly. As Ibrahim scampers down the street and disappears into the gathering mist, I see Narendra doubling over with pain and swiftly turning back to his car. Adam instinctively gets back into the car and I roll down my window and call out to my harried bootlegger.

'*Ruko*, it's me, Narendra,' I scream. But he doesn't turn to look at me. Instead, he jumps back into his car and starts the engine. As his car zooms out of the street, I stand there silently, mourning over the tragic loss of my raspberry vodka, which has left along with my fear-stricken bootlegger.

11 p.m.

'Don't worry guys,' Topsy reassures us as Adam and I enter her house. 'We have plenty of booze.'

Adam's temper has subsided. The drive to Topsy's house was fraught with silence. I was tempted to crack a lame joke about the entire episode to bring a smile to

my friend's face. My momentary angst over not getting
booze from Narendra had been replaced with concern
for Adam. But I couldn't muster the courage to commit
such sacrilege over the fresh wounds of Adam's broken
relationship. Instead, I stared in speechless amazement
as he ignored his angst by drumming his fingers on the
steering wheel. He drove his Suzuki towards Topsy's
house at a hair-raising pace. He even broke a few traffic
rules and rolled down the window to smoke though an
entire packet of cigarettes during the time it took for us
to get to Topsy's apartment.

'Thanks for having us,' Adam says as we walk into
the living room, his rage forgotten. Bilal is ensconced on
a black sofa next to the window and he already has a
drink in his hand. He wears a mournful look on his face.

'What's the matter, Bilal?' I venture to ask. 'Why do
you look so sad?'

'It's all over,' his glum voice rings through the room.
'There will be no political career. No lockdown. No
justice.'

Adam throws a facetious look at me. I suppress the
urge to laugh at Bilal's pitiable condition. Let this be
a lesson to those who think politics is the cure to all
maladies. The reality, as Bilal has come to know, is far
from enticing.

Topsy walks into the room with a bottle of champagne.
She always knows how to cheer me up.

'I think you've had enough, Billu,' says to Bilal, and
snatches the glass from his hands. For a second, the
memory of that domineering, sex-starved woman I once
knew falls away and Topsy begins to resemble a portrait

of my mother as a young wife who excels at nagging her spouse. God help me if I ever become one of those women. I'd rather die a spinster who gets no action than be a burden on a neurotic husband who can't stand the sight of me. Like Daddy, I too have standards and insist on keeping them.

'*Hai,* Tabuji,' Bilal coos. 'Don't deprive me of the only thing I have. You know I'd do anything for you. But *sharaab* is all I have.'

Topsy ignores him and begins speaking to Adam. For the rest of the evening, Billu is conveniently forgotten. He makes the black sofa his resting place for the night while Tabuji, Adam and I celebrate the end of my stint at the *Daily Image.*

30 October 2016

1.30 a.m.

'He's becoming insufferable,' Topsy confides in me after Adam leaves and Bilal passes out. 'I know he's partly done this for me. But he's miserable and making me miserable.'

'What is the matter though?' I respond tipsily. 'How did this PTI craze begin?'

'Well, Bilal was always a closet Insafian,' Topsy whispers lest Bilal wakes up and overhears her. 'Ever since the 2014 protests, he's wanted to join the party and fulfil his political aspirations. Someone from the party asked him to join last month. Bilal was already hugely inspired by the recent talk about the Panama leaks and about holding Nawaz accountable. So he joined. But his mother – who worships the PML-N – said the PTI was simply making another dramatic attempt to show that Imran has power in Punjab.'

'Oh,' I say, listening intently.

'His family pressured him to quit,' Topsy continues. 'I still can't believe he decided to quit because his mother wanted him to. For crying out loud, I told him that I won't sleep with him till he quits. Since when did mothers become more important than lovers?'

I don't see why Topsy is complaining. Bilal's mother has managed to pluck him out of the stark landscape of *dharna*s and political wrangling. What more does she want?

'I think I made a mistake,' Topsy starts whispering again. 'He drinks every night and sleeps throughout the day. He talks about the political doomsday that will begin with Nawaz's resignation. I tell you, this man needs help.'

'Why are you even bothering with him then?'

This question is not without reason. In the past, Topsy has always wriggled out of such tight spots without as much as a scab. She doesn't need to worry about men like Bilal. Zarain, her previous boyfriend, was preternaturally obsessed with Fran Drescher – I'm guessing he was one of those nineties' kids who grew up watching horrendously dubbed reruns of American sitcoms. He would expect Topsy to dress like Fran's character in *The Nanny*, and speak in her distinctly nasal voice. Topsy played along till Zarain removed the skimpy red outfit she used to wear to play the part and started trying it on for himself. But unlike Zarain, Bilal has no drastic flaws that can put Topsy off –

she is quite forgiving when her man kisses another woman and Bilal is no exception. However, when she's miserable, she has every reason to chuck him out and make space for a new man. Monogamy is overrated anyway.

'I don't want to be cruel,' she says. 'He's been incredibly supportive. I can't show him the door when he's down.'

Topsy has undoubtedly lost her sense of adventure. If it were up to me, I'd have shown Bilal the window so he could jump off and fall to the bottom. That would put an end to his misery as well.

'I see someone's falling in love,' I say. 'Maybe we should plan your trousseau.'

'Cut the crap,' Topsy hisses. 'I can't marry a miserable man like him. He just needs to drink it all off. But you tell me, how does it feel to be liberated from that god-awful place?'

Over the past few hours, I had completely forgotten that I too was coping with my own dilemmas. With friends like these, who needs enemies to distract them?

'I'm feeling stronger than I did before,' I say, though with hesitation. 'A burden has been lifted off my shoulders. I just wish I'd said goodbye to Hafeez properly.'

'Ugh, that boy is going to be trouble,' Topsy says as she lights a cigarette. 'Stay away from him. I know he's your friend. But things change very quickly between two people when one person is selfish and the other is too naïve.'

'I'm not naïve,' I say. 'I just find this whole fight between Hafeez and me to be a bit strange. It started with me attending Mopsy's wedding. How did it progress to him kissing me?'

'Well, as they say, there is no smoke without fire,' Topsy says and takes a drag of her cigarette.

I find it distressing that she chose to explain my predicament with this useless analogy. Topsy seems to be losing her spark. The nagging wife in her has hijacked the pleasantly irreverent nymph that endeared me to her. It breaks my heart to see her painful transition from a vamp to a wimp. Where will I go with my troubles now?

2 a.m.

When my Careem chauffeur drops me outside my house, I notice Dhanno parked on the other side of the road. I instinctively waddle over and knock at the window. Surpised by the sound, Hafeez pulls his hand away from the steering wheel with a jerk, rolls down the window and lets out a barely audible gasp.

'Tanya!' He wears a startled look on his face, as if he has been caught performing an espionage mission. 'Where have you been? Sonia has been worried about you. Why aren't you answering your phone?'

'Screw that,' I say with drunken indifference. 'Come inside. I'll make us some chai.'

This is getting all the more confusing. What does this man want from me? Why has he been waiting outside my house? Why do we fight and make up so easily? Am I the enabling force? Or is he deliberately seeking me out to play a pointless game of hide-and-seek? Screw it, I am too drunk to care about intentions. If I know him well, I know why he's here. And frankly, I could use some of what he has to offer.

2.15 a.m.

'I'm sorry about what happened with Hassan,' he says as he sips from a cup of chai that I made. 'I spoke to him after you left and he regrets his decision and wants you back.'

'Is that why you are here?' I demand, a drunken rage settling into my voice. 'To woo me back on his behalf? You're mighty insensitive, Hafeez. And here I thought you'd come to check up on me.'

Thank god that Mummy is asleep and Lurch is watching porn in the kitchen. I have a feeling this will escalate into one of those intense conversations. Someone will lose an arm, a leg or a sensitive organ if a scuffle breaks out.

'That's not why I came,' he says, placing the cup on the glass table with a loud clatter. He rises from the sofa and walks towards me. Gingerly, he interlocks my hands in his and caresses them with his fingers before he bends his head and kisses my hand. I feel the temptation to respond to his touch, to press my lips against his, relive the memory of the first time we kissed and make drunken love to him. But something holds me back – a fear that is much too profound and menacing to be ignored.

'What are you doing?' I ask, abruptly moving my hand away from his lips. He looks stunned.

'Tanya,' he says, staring at me with crestfallen, tearful eyes.

'What?' I hear myself say snappishly.

He turns away from me and walks out the door. I watch him leave, still perplexed by my reaction. Hafeez

hadn't done anything to deserve a Kaptaan chappal flung
at his behind or have his wine glass confiscated. Why did
I react so vehemently to him kissing my hand when his
lips have already travelled to other parts of my body?
Why am I holding back?

Of Brooms and Grooms

31 October 2016

1 p.m.

There is more to Lurch than the Mummy-loving, pakora-frying, porn-watching cook who can usually be found lounging like a *seth* instead of sleeping in the servant quarters. I often forget this inconvenient truth amid all the misplaced rage and admonition that I throw his way.

But today, as I watch Mummy haggling with him over the duration of his leave like a snooty begum sahib argues with a shopkeeper at a Sunday bazaar, I am reminded of the unspoken boundary between us and him.

'*Sirf two days*,' Mummy's voice rings in my ears. 'Not more, not less.'

Lurch lowers his head in disappointment, stymied into submission, as if a wily Mummy has confiscated his stash of Razia videos.

'Stop being fascist, Mummy. The poor chap needs a break.'

'All of us know what he does,' Mummy scoffs. 'Why give him more of an excuse?'

Mummy seems to be vacillating between two extremes of emotion again. She needs to be incarcerated already, before she murders someone in her confusion.

Lurch squats on the marble floor and watches Mummy and me arguing with each other in English. He rests his chin on his left palm and smiles with amusement as we converse in a language he doesn't understand.

'Go take time off,' I tell Lurch, defying Mummy's dictum with shameless ease. '*Ek hafta.*'

Lurch rises ecstatically to his feet, then whispers a polite and servile *shukriya.*

'Tanya!' Mummy jumps up from the sofa and puts her hands on her protruding hips. 'Ever since you've quit, you have been extra generous to the help. Take your guilt and use it to spoil someone else's *naukar*s. This house will crumble without Haji.'

'And so will you,' I say, pointing a finger at her. 'You'll never be the same again.' Much as the blind bat has a tendency to exaggerate, she does have a point. The insecurity of sudden unemployment has made me strangely sensitive. It can get difficult to journey without a map. You either tend to fall into the trap of wandering aimlessly until you find a convenient destination or you make frequent pit stops in search of destiny.

'If you're so concerned about the rights of the *naukar*s, why don't you do something to protect them rather than lying on your lazy bum all day?' Mummy responds in a waspish tone that aggravates me.

'As they say, Mummy, charity – like all other calamities – begins at home,' I say in a petulant voice.

'So *bechara* Haji is your first experiment,' she says, missing the sarcasm embedded in my words.

'It'll work in my favour.' I scan through a magazine lying on the table next to the sofa. 'If I manage to speak up about his rights, there is a very strong likelihood that you'll be sent to prison.'

'Hah,' she hollers. 'Good luck with that. *Beta*, your mind has become the devil's plaything since you...'

I look up from the magazine and glare at her.

'Say it, Mummy,' I raise my voice. 'Say it ... since I refused to become Hassan's plaything.'

'*Tauba*, you're hopeless.' Mummy taps her hands against her forehead.

'All I'm saying is that you need to get a new job.'

'I have a new job,' I whack the magazine against the sofa. 'I've been asked to write a column for an Indian publication.'

'What?' Mummy bellows. 'And you're going to do it?'

'Chill, Mummy, you're overreacting. It's not like I'm marrying a Hindu boy. I'm just writing for his publication. His name is Inder. We were briefly involved.'

'*Ab samjhi main.*' Mummy nods accusingly, as if my reasons for telling her about the *Time and Beyond* piece have a more furtive source. 'It's because of that Indian boy. He's made you quit the *Daily Image* and is recruiting you for his anti-Pakistan cause.'

'Mummy,' my voice quivers with impatience. 'He's not recruiting me for anything. He's just a friend.'

This is entirely untrue. Over the past few weeks, my
relationship with Inder has evolved into one of those
mundane writer-editor connections. We no longer share the
silence-spattered intimacy that comes with being former
lovers. The initial clumsiness of Inder's efforts to harmlessly
flirt with me has ebbed. He adopts a cold demeanour with
me because he's started seeing a girl from Pune. Inder's
enthusiasm for the *Time and Beyond* piece has endured the
test of time and the mercurial shifts in his mood.

'What does he want you to write about?' Mummy
backs down after she realizes that I'm angry. After I told
her off two days ago, Mummy has been careful about
what she says and does.

'It's an article about the change in attitudes towards
India in Pakistan after the situation worsened in Kashmir
this summer,' I reply after a brief interlude. 'He wants me
to capture the mood of the times.'

'He wants you to make it easier for them to spy on us,'
Mummy snaps a reply. 'He wants to know our secrets.'

'What secrets can I provide him?' I rise from the sofa.
'How can I, an unemployed subeditor who spends her
days immured in her palatial home like a modern-day
Anarkali, tell him anything? Knowing me, I'd misread
the temperature and instigate yet another civil war in the
region.'

Mummy chuckles, as if she tacitly acknowledges my
ability to start a war.

'Jokes aside, my concerns are legitimate, *beta*.'
Mummy's low voice indicates her fear. 'Why don't you
tell someone else to write it?'

That's not a bad idea. Sonia has the knack to compose a good story – even if she can't do justice to it. Khirad, when she was still reporting for the *Daily Image*, also had similar traits. Her mind was brimming with curiosity over the nature and ambit of her stories, even if she struggled to give them the right shape.

'You're right,' I bounce back on the sofa and prop my feet on its arm. 'As it is, my role at the *Daily Image* was to polish these stories. I was the middleman, the fall guy, the ayah who took responsibility for a child that wasn't my own and got paid for it.'

'My poor *beti*. Always the ayah, never the memsahib,' Mummy taunts me but I ignore her.

'And when I worked on my own stories, I found a way to let my biases seep into my reportage,' I respond wistfully. 'And Inder wanted me of all people to understand the tensions from my selective view. Does he even care about the truth?'

Mummy smiles smugly. She seems to have talked me out of writing the piece and she knows it. '*Shukar hain*, now get a job and stop spoiling my servant.'

'Mummy, let the poor chap be for a while,' I tell her. 'He also needs a break.'

'I need a break,' she says, plopping herself on the sofa and stretching her arms in the air. 'No one gives *me* a *hafta* off. *Hai*, I should go for *umrah* this year.'

'Oh wow, I can't believe you found a way to slide your annual trips to the Holy Land into the conversation.'

'Nonsense, *beta*,' Mummy responds, knowing in her heart that most of her reasons for hopping on a flight to

Jeddah seem to be inspired by silly cliches and feigned piety. '*Allah ka bulawa aata hai mujhe.*'

I scoff in disbelief. 'As if god has the time to write invitation letters to you every year,' I say. 'Why not send Lurch this time?'

'Why? So I can miss all the fun?' Mummy's words are soaked in a fiery vengeance, as if she were bitter about a fresh wound. They prick as easily as they bleed. Her sensitivity and defensiveness makes me doubt whether she has been going to Saudi Arabia for all these years. I suspect that she has been taking time off to visit a new exotic destination every year.

'Don't be silly, Mummy,' I say, trying to give her the benefit of the doubt. 'There's only so much fun you can have when you visit the same place every year.'

The phone rings and Lurch hurriedly answers it.

'Tanya baby, it's for you,' he says, clutching the receiver between his knuckles. 'Sonia *baji.*'

In an age when technology is breaking barriers between people and places, Sonia finds ways to retain her backwardness. Why can't she call me on my cell phone? This woman always finds new ways to infuriate me. Next time she's upset with me, I'll let her be. I could use some normalcy these days. Maybe silence and a vacation will fix me right up.

1.10 p.m.

'Hi T,' Sonia says, panting as though she's just run a marathon. 'Sorry I called you on your landline. My phone died and I could only remember your landline number. I just couldn't wait to tell you this.'

The excitement in Sonia's voice should make me curious about what she wants to tell me. But over time, I've become accustomed to Sonia's bouts of enthusiasm. Nothing she says or does fazes me anymore. Even at the height of her journalistic powers, Sonia fails to file stories that can inspire any emotions within me apart from irritation. If we were lovers, I'd be cold towards her every night, my body unaffected by her touch.

'Tanya,' she pauses. 'Saad and his wife are getting divorced.'

'What? When?' My heart races at such a feverish pace that I fear it will eventually stop beating. This is the first time Sonia has given me news that has shocked me. If only she could do that with one of her stories. She'd have a successful career to look forward to in addition to her ex-fiancé's broken marriage.

'I'll come over and give you details,' Sonia says before I can ask her more.

2 p.m.

'It's true,' Topsy tells me over the phone. 'Mopsy left him. I know he wants to believe otherwise.'

'Was it because she wasn't satisfied in the bedroom?' I giggle like a schoolgirl. 'He did have a tendency to be spent before time.'

'It's not just that,' Topsy says excitedly. 'Mopsy thinks he's too meek. She needs a man, not a mouse.'

'Meanwhile, Sonia's on her way here to give me details,' I say. 'She seems thrilled.'

'Well, she shouldn't get her hopes up,' Topsy's voice drops to a whisper. 'I hear Saad has his eye on another woman.'

'Does it really matter? I'm sure Sonia just felt wronged and now wants to see him suffer.'

'Let's hope,' Topsy responds cryptically. 'Meanwhile, Bilal is still in mourning over quitting PTI. It's sickening. I've decided to follow Mopsy's lead and leave him.'

It's truly the season for disunity. Everyone is breaking away from some restrictive alliance or the other. I've left the *Daily Image*. Mopsy has bounced Saad out the door. Topsy is losing her patience with Bilal. I wonder who's going to be next to fall victim to this season of senseless heartbreak. Please let it be Hassan. I'm sure he has a new girlfriend who's willing to get rid of him. If not, I wish Bina sells the house and divorces him for a younger man. Now that would be the best form of revenge.

'Good for you, babe,' I say. 'What made you take this decision?'

'When you left that night, Bilal woke up and started talking about PTI's plans for Pakistan's *tabdeeli*. I don't usually date people for their political beliefs. Nor do I leave them for it. But somehow, I felt no respect for him or his vision. No measure of good sex can compensate for this.'

I was right when I thought Bilal was turning Topsy into a fool. She has lost her sense of identity in this relationship. Even sex can't save them now.

'Wow, Topsy,' I make a fervent attempt to sound supportive. 'I guess you're growing up.'

'You're right,' Topsy laughs. 'But who said sex won't have the same effect on me? Also, Bilal should consider himself lucky that my law firm decided against defending Nawaz in the Panama leaks case. He and I would have been fighting constantly if the firm had agreed to take it on.'

For the first time since Khalid left and Bilal waltzed into her life, I notice that Topsy has a way of deflecting attention from the vulnerable aspects of her life. She, like me, has the ability to laugh the pain away. And I thought only I was capable of doing this.

2.40 p.m.

'Tanya, *meri jaan*,' Sonia hugs me as she walks in. 'I'm just so relieved that this happened to him.'

Sonia seems to have developed a sadistic streak over the weeks when we weren't speaking to each other. Frankly, if you look beyond the bitterness and resentment, you begin to realize that she is genuinely funny. I wouldn't go to the extent of suggesting that she can try her luck at a stand-up routine, but she has the verve and intensity to be a funny person on occasion.

'Why are you so excited though?' I ask as we make our way into my bedroom. 'You don't think he's going to run back to you, do you?'

'Don't be silly, T,' Sonia says, jumping on to my bed and resting her elbow on a backrest pillow like she used to when she would visit me during our college days. 'I am just happy that he now realizes how I've suffered.'

When Sonia mentions her suffering, guilt wracks my heart and courses through my veins with poisonous intensity. I try to suppress it, to fight the urge to conceal the truth, to keep her from knowing my insidious role in the story of her heartbreak. But I've never been much of a war strategist and the words roll off my tongue with clarity.

'Sonia, I went to Mopsy and Saad's wedding,' I confess, sitting on the sofa so that I'm at a safe distance from Sonia in case she loses it. 'I'm sorry. It wasn't right of me to do that. I thought that if I went there to talk to Saad, I could tell him that it was wrong of him to jilt you on your wedding night and that he owed you an apology face to face. And I did but I don't know if he took it seriously.'

For a few seconds, silence fills the room like an unwanted intruder. Sonia's body freezes against the backrest pillow. I'm tempted to walk over towards her and check if she has turned to stone – I'm not Medusa but I have been known to have the same effect on men. But I'm much too afraid after the sandal fiasco.

The silence is shattered by a gentle knock on the door. Lurch pops his head in through the door, still smiling about the generous holiday package I've offered him.

'Baby, *Saad sahib aaye hain*,' he says with a toothless smile that makes me recoil in horror. What the hell? Talk about timing.

Sonia jumps to her feet and dashes towards me. Instinctively, I shield my head with my hands. But Sonia doesn't attack me.

'What's Saad doing here, Tanya?' she asks, confusion in her eyes.

'I have no idea, Sonia,' I assure her. 'But don't you worry. If you don't want him here, I'll ask him to leave at once. How dare he just waltz into my house?'

'Listen,' she says, her words seeded with an inexplicable excitement and playfulness. 'Go meet him. I'll be waiting by the stairs.'

'I'll do it,' I say. 'As long as you don't abandon me, I'll do it. Just make sure this isn't like one of your causes that you forget. Remember what happened when you tried to mobilize all the maids in your neighbourhood to fight for their rights?'

'Don't worry,' Sonia assures me. 'I won't abandon you like I abandoned those *jamadaarni*s. Don't worry at all.'

When Sonia had called off the movement, a group of women cleaners and ayahs arrived at her doorstep and thrashed her with brooms. But this time around, I'm the one who's in the line of fire. What if she changes her mind midway and falls into her ex-fiancé's arms? I don't even know where Lurch keeps the brooms in the kitchen. If she decides to change her allegiances, I'll have to bear the consequences all by myself. Have I made a mistake by agreeing to do this?

'Let's hope this time Karl Marx won't give in to the capitalists and become one of the wretched bourgeoisie,' I say as Sonia pushes me out of my room.

3 p.m.

'I love you, Tanya,' Saad exclaims, holding my fingers in his rough hands. 'I can't live without you. No woman can erase the memory of the night we spent together. Please come with me. We can get married.'

How do people have the temerity to walk into my house and say whatever comes to mind? I should slap this man for asking me such a silly question. Why would I marry a man like him? There's a difference between a stolen good and a used good. As it is, Tanya Shaukat doesn't wear hand-me-downs.

In Saad's case, the boundaries have been blurred to the extent that they don't even exist. Not only is he a used good, but – after Mopsy snatched him from Sonia – he is also stolen good. Why should I settle for a *chori ka maal* that has someone else's fingerprints on it?

'I know I've been unfair to Sonia and Mehnaz,' Saad continues. 'You might think that I'm one hell of a player. I'm sure you do. But since the night of my wedding reception, when you went to that shady corner with that asshole in the grey suit, I haven't been able to get you out of my mind.'

Saad clenches his fist and waves it in the air to emphasize his point. While he speaks, I gaze into his teary eyes – is he wearing glycerin?

'Tanya,' Saad blurts out my name with urgency. 'Aren't you going to say anything? I've just confessed my love to you. Surely, you have something to say about that, no?'

I'm just staring at him as he says all these things. I'm too shocked to react. How do I react to this imbecile's rubbish? He's been shifting from one woman to the other like we're part of a Rolodex. Saad's glorified sense of entitlement will land him in trouble one of these days. What did Sonia and Mopsy see in this egotistical twat? Better still, what did I see in him? I should have exercised better drunken judgement and chucked him out like a used cigarette when I had the chance. Mummy is right when she says that when the undeserving are allowed access to a diamond, they don't know what to do with it and eventually let it slip into the wrong hands. That's how she explains the loss of the Kohinoor and complains

about how my independence has made me prone to
frequent lapses of judgement.

Saad pauses and sighs. 'Please say something. I can't
bear this silence. It's killing me.'

Does this fool genuinely expect me to believe that my
silence is killing him? He ought to know that my silence
is reserved for more menacing pursuits. If I had any
murderous intentions towards Saad, silence wouldn't be
my weapon of choice. I'd search for Bakhtu Bhai, borrow
his axe and use it to commit a noble deed.

'Let's discuss this over dinner,' he says, attempting to
get me to engage. 'We could go watch a movie at the
Nueplex Cinema or the Cinepax at Ocean Mall. Maybe
that new Karan Johar movie, *Ae Dil Hai Muslim.* I mean
Mushkil.'

'You seem to be torn between a glorious past and an
inglorious present,' I say. My words are dipped in venom
and peppered with the kind of *mirchi* that can leave
people's tongues burning for days.

'Pardon me?' His eyes twitch in confusion.

'No Indian movies are being shown at local cinemas
after the finger-pointing match with India,' I say. 'Even if
a rebellious multiplex owner decided to defy regulations
and screen a film from across the border, *Ae Dil Hai
Mushkil* wouldn't feature among his top choices.'

'Is it not?' Saad knits his eyebrows, looking pensive.
'Not even at the old cinemas in Saddar? Bambino?
Nishat?'

His ignorance angers me.

'If you weren't caught up being a philandering fool
who changes women at the speed you change underwear,

you'd know this,' I click my tongue to shame him for being so blissfully unaware. 'You'd also know that Nishat burnt down many years ago.'

But Saad is unfazed by the remark. He seems to be decidedly loyal to me for some peculiar reason.

'I just felt the theme was suitable,' he smiles. 'It's about unrequited love. Losing love. The way I lost you.'

This is getting slightly out of hand. I'll have to deal with him in my own way. And it won't be a pleasant sight.

'Saad, *meri jaan*,' I say cloyingly and begin stroking his chin with my fingers. 'To lose something, you must first gain it.'

'Did I not gain you that night?' he moves closer to me. 'Did we not become one that night?'

'*Nahi, meri jaan*,' I say, imitating Razia's voice from Lurch's movie – of course I watched it. 'As you said, *ae dil hai Muslim*.'

Saad chuckles loudly, as if he has never heard a funnier joke in his life. In a fit of wild enthusiasm, he moves his lips close to mine. Driven by my urge to get revenge for Sonia, I succumb to his wet, clumsy kiss. However, like a true warrior, I keep one eye open and stare up at the staircase to signal Sonia. I catch sight of her peeping down the stairwell with her hand cupped against her mouth, the disapproval in her eyes making her pupils dilate.

I knew I couldn't trust her to follow my cue, to act instinctively and help me shame this twat once and for all. Her feelings and misplaced prejudices always manage to spill into everything and create a colossal mess. Now she'll think this was all a staged ploy to make her jealous and never speak to me again. Ugh, Sonia is so predictable.

Reluctant to give up so easily, I attempt to make her understand that my lack of resistance to Saad is part of the plan to humiliate him. Between wrestling with Saad's tongue and pressing my left hand against his shoulder – if only that alone could kill him – I wave my free hand in Sonia's direction.

Within seconds, she runs down the stairs, creeps up behind Saad and flings a *jharoo* at his head. Fortunately, I had seen her coming down the stairs and had extricated myself from Saad mere seconds before Sonia attacked him. I didn't expect her to launch her offensive with such tact. If she tries hard enough, Sonia can be full of surprises. I don't even know how she found the *jharoo* so quickly.

'How dare you!' Sonia bellows as she hits the *jharoo* against his wavy hair. 'You have some nerve walking into this house and proposing to my friend like that. Have you no shame?'

'Sonia ... baby ... stop ... you know I was playing ... it's always been you. I've always wanted you.'

'What?' I say with mock anger. 'But you just told me that you loved me. How can you love the both of us at once?'

A ghostly pallor appears on Saad's face as he wipes a layer of dust from his hair. His body stiffens as he struggles to plan his next move.

'Do us a favour,' I put my arm around his shoulder – the same one I'd caressed with my hand a few minutes ago – and walk him towards the main door. 'Take your shit elsewhere. Perhaps to someone who cares.'

As Saad steps out of the door, Sonia throws the *jharoo* at him once again. He tries to duck but miscalculates the distance between the door and the steps in front of it and stumbles. A cobweb that resembles a long, misshapen strand of hair, hangs from his head as he dashes out of the gate, gets into his car and drives away. As Sonia and I lock the door, the thunderous roar of his engine blends with the distant sound of honking cars and a sea breeze whistling through the palm trees in my neighbour's garden. By the time we reach the stairs, the sounds die out and a gentle calm fills the air.

5 p.m.

'You know something, Tanya…' Sonia says as I roll a joint in my room.

Much as I adore her for delivering a stellar performance and helping me get rid of Saad, Sonia must realize that we aren't telepathic. I can't sense her pain, insecurities and thoughts without this special link. And frankly, I don't think I want to have such a deep, depressing connection with Sonia.

'What is it?' I ask with forced politeness.

'I was afraid you were going to give in,' she says, twitching her eyes to hold back tears. 'I feared that you would marry Saad and abandon our friendship.'

'Well, contrary to what you've thought all along, I am a good friend,' I say as I roll my eyes. 'Besides, I wouldn't even want to end up with a man like Saad at gunpoint. Sleeping with him was a drunken mistake … a curse. Today, I've broken the curse. I was just worried about you, though.'

'Me?' Sonia looks perplexed. 'Why would you worry about me?'

'I was concerned that you'd give in to your emotions and switch sides,' I say, taking a drag of my joint.

Sonia giggles until a throaty laugh forms in her mouth and takes its place.

'What's so funny?'

Sonia isn't known for being the laughing sort. Not even a smile can last long on her characteristically crestfallen face.

'Why would I care about him?' Sonia points to the window as if Saad has returned and set up camp outside my room. 'I have a fiancé. I can't two-time like a certain someone.'

'Wait. What? When? Who's the un ... I mean ... lucky guy? Do I know him?'

After a while, journalists lose the ability to be fazed by breaking news. With time, they attribute this quality to everyone around them. Sonia is yet another prisoner to this strange habit. Though as I said earlier, she has generally been unable to surprise me much ... until today.

'Why didn't you mention this earlier?'

'T, I wanted to be careful,' she hisses like a snake. 'I didn't want anything to go wrong. Anyway, I'm planning the wedding for July.'

She rises to her feet and clutches her purse.

'And where do you think you're going?' I ask as she makes her way out the door.

'I have a couple of errands to run,' Sonia says, making every attempt to avoid eye contact with me. 'I must get on it right away. There's so much to do. So little time.'

'Sonia,' I interrupt. 'Who's the groom? Don't be so evasive.'

Sonia runs down the stairs, as if she were escaping from prison, and I follow her. At first, she resembles a coy bride whose wedding veil has accidentally slipped and fallen. But when we reach the front door, I realize that she isn't blushing or embarrassed. Her lips are tightly pressed and she looks nervous. She's hiding something. I can always tell when she's concealing the truth. The woman is much too transparent to keep a secret.

'You know him,' Sonia says as she hurriedly walks out of the door. 'It's Hafeez.'

My heart gallops as Sonia rushes out of the gate, jumps into her mother's white Corolla and zooms past the same sights and sounds that had greeted – or should I say mocked – Saad on his journey home not too long ago. Tears roll down my cheeks as I lock the front door and return to my room.

Typically Tanya

31 October 2016

7 p.m.

A shade of purple spreads through the sky outside my window, and patches of grey foreshadow the promise of night. I haven't bothered to switch the lights on inside my room. I bury myself under a duvet until its crumpled surface feels snug against my skin and envelops me in darkness.

I think I'm coming down with something. My knees have stiffened. My body is shaking. A gnawing ache is coursing through my body. Is this the moment when fate draws with Tanya Shaukat and throws her out of the ring?

At times like these, it is questions that have the most damaging effect on me. They inhabit my mind like a posse of distant relatives who never leave. Unfortunately, I can't issue eviction notices to my thoughts. And right now, I can't control them as they stream through my mind.

Why am I so upset about this debacle? Is it the element of surprise or something more lethal that is making my heart race? Am I distraught that Hafeez is marrying Sonia – the woman I've always considered to be inferior to me? No. Maybe. I don't know. It all seems so shocking, so surreal. Sonia and Hafeez? The notion is raw and repulsive and makes me flinch with disgust.

As I lie in bed, another thought drops into my mind like a missile – what will happen when Sonia gets to know that Hafeez and I have been fooling around in a vague yet dangerous capacity? Sonia will find a way to slaughter me to pieces. I can't afford to get into trouble again. I need to stop reacting in such an emotional manner. I'm not someone who gets fazed by these things and I'm not the sort to feel betrayed – especially when the traitor isn't even my lover.

I wait for sleep to clasp me in its warm embrace. I'd do anything to break away from this spiral of pain. But at this moment, sleep doesn't come to me easily. There is a barrier, an unsettling pain that is keeping it at a distance. Sleep may have knocked on the doors and windows of my mind, only to find itself barred by my questions without answers. They have bolted all the doors and I am now trapped in a world of insecurity.

7.30 p.m.

The tragedy of having friends like mine is that they always disappoint me when I need them the most. I frantically dial Topsy's number. But much to my consternation, she keeps rejecting the call, as if I am one of those infamous blank-callers who has mastered the art of pestering unsuspecting victims over the phone. For a while, I feel hopelessly unwanted.

Topsy replies a few minutes later. 'With Bilal. He seems to be in a terrible place. I'll get back to you soon.'

I guess I can forgive her for not being here for me. After all, breaking an Insafian's heart is a noble deed. Who am I to come between a woman and her struggle for freedom?

7.36 p.m.

Khirad answers her phone after the third ring.

'Babe, I'm on my way to the airport,' she says, sounding preoccupied. 'Going to Isloo to cover the whole Imran lockdown fiasco. All good?'

Driven by a selfish instinct, I tell Khirad the entire story with impressive speed. She listens patiently and lets out a loud gasp.

'I never thought he would do this,' she says, outrage in her voice. 'He reminds me of Hassan. Kiss him goodbye forever. Good riddance.'

Before I can respond to her, Khirad announces that she has arrived at the airport and will call me from Islamabad once she has free time.

When she hangs up, I decide to message Adam. His response is swift and shocking.

'At Ibrahim's,' he writes. 'Came here to talk things out with him. Don't worry, I'm not getting back together with him. I just want to be there for him. He seems lonely what with all the pressure he's been under to get married. He needs a friend.'

Adam enjoys being Mother Teresa. But he needs to be a bit more selective about his causes or he'll get hurt again.

8 p.m.

Since none of my friends can counsel me, I decide to take action and text Hafeez. My message is clear. It is not laced with hidden meanings and innuendo. I don't want to play any more mind games with him. This has to end and I need answers to my questions.

'Meet me tomorrow morning. I need to talk. And don't cancel on me. This is important.'

I send the message without a hint of emotion. After a while, indifference becomes an elixir for the soul. It gives me the courage to hedge away unwanted aggression and hide in a protective shell until I'm prepared to embrace facts and confront reality.

8.30 p.m.

'This is a terrible time, Inder,' I shout into the receiver. 'I'll call you back.'

'Oh, I just wanted to ask about the piece,' he says, his low voice laced with warmth and sincerity. 'Time's running out, baby.'

'Inder, I'm not sure if I'm the right person to write that piece,' I respond, slightly calmer than before. 'I wouldn't want to write something that is untrue. You are expecting me to write a piece about the common man. But I really can't tell a story that I know so little about.'

'Isn't that selfish?' Inder's incriminatory tone pricks at my conscience. For a second, I doubt my own intentions.

'Aren't you a journalist? Shouldn't you be unraveling these facts and presenting them to the public?'

'Let me explain,' I say, exhaling loudly before I clarify my stance. 'We, as journalists, can only peel back a few layers of a person's life. I can question my way into his or her experiences but to an extent. If I take on this piece, I fear that I won't be able to represent people's true perceptions on Burhan Wani's death, Uri and beyond.'

'That's absurd,' Inder says with distrust. 'You live there. You should know what's going on and what people think.'

'Class differences will always keep these experiences alien and strange for someone like me,' I say. 'When you don't belong, you can't admit to know.'

'So you're saying there's a wall between your world and the world I'm telling you to understand,' he says.

'It's not a wall, Inder,' I pipe up. 'It's a whole other world.'

I pause, as if to be praised for the depth of my thoughts. When he fails to acknowledge my shameless attempt to win praise, I continue with my explanation. But I can tell that something has changed. Inder's silence is fraught with meaning, a thought that is still setting its parameters in his mind.

'Uri and perhaps even Burhan Wani's death will never affect people in radical terms,' I say. 'It will only have an effect in political and diplomatic circles. And there is always a class difference when it comes to being affected by ground realities. Why would the privileged upper class care about atrocities in Kashmir? It's all so remote from their lives.'

'Ah, you seem to have a point,' Inder responds politely, as if he is pretending to listening to me.

'Such events have always receded into the background,' I tell him, sounding all the more preachy. 'We all know how news cycles function. A scandal bubbles to the surface until it is popped by another pressing story. Amid all these conflicting news cycles, the people lose sight of what they should prioritize. It doesn't even matter to anyone. When the backdrop is so remote, why will there even be a need to prioritize it?'

'What kind of story do you want to tell?' Inder asks. 'What story will your heart be willing to tell?'

I find myself battling the urge to laugh at the cheesy manner in which Inder asks the question. But a new thought forms in my mind when he asks that question. The idea is irresistible and wickedly irreverent in equal measure. Although the notion has just dropped into my mind and hasn't even found a comfortable crevice in which to rest its head, I feel the need to share it with Inder in its raw form.

'I want to write about the indifference,' I say. Inder remains silent. His silence is a licence for me to continue, to construct the skeleton of an idea that has yet to morph into something that will interest him.

'Then write that,' Inder says suddenly, as if he has just woken up from deep slumber and realized he was expected to respond. 'Document how socioeconomic factors and an apolitical approach shape our response to such events.'

'I can't document that,' I say, adding another melodramatic dialogue to my warehouse of scriptwriting gems. 'I am also a victim of this myopic attitude. How can I propose to explain anything about the society I live in when I belong to a tiny segment of the elite?'

'Tanya, you're a genius!' Inder shouts as if he's found gold under his pillow. 'You should write us a weekly column that is told from the perspective of a clueless woman from Karachi's elite, which tells these personal stories about what's happening across the border.'

'But doesn't that also fall into the category of "elitist complaints"? I thought...'

'Not when it's written in a satirical manner,' he cuts me off. 'You're capable of being funny. You could work on being empathetic, though. But you'll learn. All I know is that you'll be the perfect person to write a column like this. You're catty and brutally honest. You can strip everyone and everything to the bone.'

Inder is really taking the idea to another level.

'Let's call it "Typically Tanya",' he continues. 'Your column for *Time and Beyond*. The editors were looking for something refreshing. Why not give them something that'll have an impact?'

'It sounds catchy and promising,' I stutter. 'But I'm slightly sceptical about it.'

'Why?' Inder sounds disappointed. 'What's on your mind?'

'You see, to strip anyone else to the bone, I'll have to be stark naked myself – a dangerous proposition in an Islamic republic. And I don't want to stigmatize or vilify anyone in the process of being funny.'

'Then create your own boundaries and parameters,' Inder says. 'You have my support.'

'Are you sure you aren't trying to take advantage of a Pakistani girl by spying on her thoughts?' I respond facetiously. 'Is this your way to win back Kulbhushan or claim Kashmir? Should I be contacting the authorities before I say yes?'

Inder's voice dissolves into laughter. He sounds like a villain from a terrible Indian movie where every punch is followed by irritating acoustics.

'There's nothing to spy on, baby,' he says flirtatiously. Then, seeming to remember that our relationship is a professional one, he changes his tone. 'I've seen what I have to see. Send your column by next Friday. Let's say 1,000 words? Don't forget. We'll be waiting for your piece.'

When he hangs up, I am assailed by doubts yet I feel a peculiar sense of contentment. Unable to control this conflicting array of emotions, I decide to crawl into bed and sleep off the trauma of losing someone and the ecstasy of gaining what may be my biggest break. After all the tremors that I've experienced today, sleep better not evade me like it did a couple of hours ago. Fortunately for me, it doesn't.

A Season of Splits

1 November 2016

2 p.m.

Koel Cafe, with its alabaster white furniture and leafy frangipani trees, has been my usual haunt in the city. For years, it's been my tiny, soundproof idyll in an otherwise grim world.

Over time, I have come here with friends, foes, hoes and bros. I have sneaked into the adjoining art gallery with a date. I've stolen a kiss under the staircase that snakes its way to the kurta shop. I've even broken up with boring, boisterous men at the cafe while eating mozzarella sticks and gulping down a chilled glass of shikanjabeen that is always too sweet.

But today, as I enter the cafe, I'm angry. My mind is wrestling with emotions that I can neither explain nor control. I pull up a chair at the table next to the door lest I have to storm out on short notice. One should always be prepared for a natural disaster and the aftermath of a dramatic confrontation. And you can never be too careful in either scenario.

'Should I bring your usual?' A waiter recognizes me and flashes a broad, blinding smile in my direction. 'Green tea.'

I nod. He takes a bow and grins. As he disappears into the kitchen, an old Coke Studio song distracts me. Zeb and Faakhir's 'Dilruba na raazi' is playing in the cafe and it momentarily pacifies me. My insecurities and fears return as Hafeez wanders in through the antique doors.

2.30 p.m.

'I did it because of you, T,' he says.

Hafeez's words are at once flattering and incriminatory. I'm not sure if I've just won a Pulitzer or if I've been handed the death penalty. He has a way with words that's completely unpredictable. It's as though these lines come to him in a moment of rare inspiration and elude him till later. In his attempts to preserve them, he manages to save those phrases that, when put together, have a dual meaning. That's what I hate the most about him.

'What do you mean?' I ask, shocked by the gravity of his words. 'Why would you decide to marry Sonia because of me?'

Hafeez buries his face into his hands. My questions have either left him fatigued or coerced him to accept a reality that he had skilfully hidden from me all this time. As his face emerges from the cage of his fingers, I detect a teardrop flowing down his cheek. Mummy has warned me to be sceptical of men who break down without any qualms. But Hafeez is an exception to the rule, if not a new rule altogether. I should be able to trust him. He's my friend – and standards of propriety vary in these situations.

Just then, the waiter arrives with my cup of green tea and a slight smile plastered on his face. I thank him and then look at Hafeez. Had it been any other man, he would have briskly looked down to conceal his tears. But he continues to stare wistfully into my eyes. His tearful glance leaves me cold with fear. It is filled with meaning – a pain which he expects me to understand. Witnessing the intensity of our wordless conversation, the waiter checks his impulse to appear overly enthusiastic. His smile wilts along the edges and then disappears. He hurriedly brings a cup of tea for Hafeez as well and makes himself scarce for the rest of the afternoon.

'Hafeez,' I say, affectionately taking his hand into mine when the waiter disappears. 'What's wrong? Why are you crying?'

'You just don't get it, do you?' Hafeez pulls his hand away. 'I'm with Sonia because of you. Because I couldn't be with someone like you, even though you were all I wanted to be with.'

Chalo, as long as there's been a confession, I have been vindicated. I'm just glad he had the courage to admit to his feelings. Come to think of it, that's possibly all I ever wanted.

'And why couldn't you be with me?' I ask smugly. 'What was holding you back from asking me what I thought or felt about you?'

'It's just the way you are,' Hafeez bellows at first, then slowly and self-consciously lowers his voice to a murmur. 'You're self-contained, selfish and aren't made for love or even marriage. Since your father walked out, you've lost the power to love and maintain a relationship with anyone. Friends and family have no real meaning in your life. You can sleep with a man and then mock him for his small parts. But something prevents you from going deeper than that to explore the possibilities of a stronger connection.'

'So why am I all you want to be with?' I ask, making sure that I sound as sarcastic as possible.

'Because I can't resist you,' he says, a radiant sparkle in his eyes. 'That's why I kept coming to you. I'd have weak moments when I'd desire you and couldn't resist myself. And yet, you were my friend and that was a reality we couldn't look beyond. That day on *chand raat*, I wanted us to spend time together. I wanted us to go for coffee. I'd finally mustered the courage to discuss my feelings with you. But when I realized that you were at Saad's wedding that night, a part of me starting hating you.'

His words take me back to those brief spells of intimacy in my house. Hafeez's passion and his desire for me were driven by ambiguity. It seems as though his mind and heart were caught in a deadly collision each time he had kissed me. Both bouts of intimacy had inspired a new confrontation and redefined the parameters of Hafeez's pain.

For a second, I feel sorry for him. But there is also a war within me. I have to address my concerns too. I want him to understand how I feel about this.

'But why did you even approach me? If you thought I was some unfeeling bitch with daddy issues, why did you make the effort to come to me in the dead of night? Why did you kiss me and simultaneously ignore me? What pleasure did you derive from being hot and cold? I don't even understand what happened here. First you were angry at me for going to Saad and Mopsy's wedding. And then you got angry because of Inder. Later, you made pit stops at my house and kissed me. All of this makes no sense, especially after your decision to marry Sonia.'

'I've said what I had to say,' he responds abruptly. 'I am marrying her because it will give me stability. I came to you because I was drawn to you. I always have been. Everything about you interests me. That's why I always had high expectations from our friendship. But now, I guess there's nothing more we can do instead of moving on and pretending this never happened.'

This man is unbelievably daft. He seems to be talking to the voice in his head. My questions and insecurities have no bearing on him. Hafeez has already made up his mind.

'Why are you making this sound like a break-up, Hafeez? It's mighty insensitive of you. I've always treated you like a friend. I admit that I do find you attractive. But I never thought you'd be reaching out to me for sex while wooing Sonia on the side. You were the mediating force between us. How could you?'

'Sonia and I grew close spontaneously,' he pauses and sips his tea. 'It's almost like your absence from our lives made it easier for us to mingle and connect on a different level. With you, I always had to try. With Sonia, trying didn't seem necessary. Everything fell into place.'

'So it was convenience that you were seeking?'

'I hate to admit it. But that's probably all I wanted. A hassle-free, happy ending. I've been hurt in the past. I'm not going to allow myself to fall into that trap again.'

'And I would have put you in that trap?'

'I didn't know what you'd put me in,' Hafeez says, raising both his hands in the air. 'You're dangerous. Moody. Manipulative. Impulsive. I could never deal with these traits.'

I grab my cup of green tea and prepare to fling it at him. If Adam can thrash Ibrahim with a Kaptaan chappal and Sonia can hit Saad with a *jharoo*, why should I hold back? After all, I'm human too. When anger strikes, it propels one to bite. Why should I stand in its way?

But Tanya Shaukat knows better than to get herself into an indelicate situation in a public place. If I throw scalding tea at him, he will have proof for all those lies that he believes about me. Plus, he'd have a reason to do the same to me and I'm not carrying an extra pair of clothes to change into afterwards.

My friend Hafeez would have understood and ignored any indecorous conduct on my part. But the man sitting next to me is no equivalent to the Hafeez I once knew and admired. They might be the same person, but there is a callousness to him that makes me cringe.

'Does Sonia know about what has been happening between us?' I ask, keeping my cup on the saucer without so much as a clatter.

'Yes, she does.' He takes another sip of his tea. 'And she understands. You know why? Because she's a good friend and doesn't want to ruin things with you. You'll see, she won't even bring it up with you.'

I rise from my seat and grab my bag.

'Thanks for meeting me,' I say, whispering as I reach out to hug him. 'I have to go...'

'Tanya,' he holds my wrist as I extricate myself from his embrace. 'Don't go. Please. I didn't mean any of that. I don't know what came over me.'

Tears roll down his cheeks. The waiter walks towards us with the bill, having noticed that we are ready to leave. I hand him a crisp thousand-rupee bill to cover our tab.

'Hafeez,' I say, wiping away another teardrop that has carelessly escaped from my eyes. 'It doesn't matter. Move on with your life. You're better off without an influence like me.'

I remove his hand from my wrist and walk out of the restaurant.

As I reach the antique door, I overhear a conversation between two waiters that amuses me.

'*Madam ne apne boyfriend ko dump kar dia,*' one of them says to the other.

'*Isi laiq hoga,*' the other waiter whispers.

At least they appreciate what I've done – even if they don't know how difficult it was for me to walk away from someone who once understood the quiet workings of my mind.

3.30 p.m.

As soon as I get into my Careem, I call Khirad and launch into a long tirade against Hafeez.

'I think you did the right thing,' she says. 'But can I call you later?'

'All good? Are you schmoozing with the creme de la creme of Isloo?'

'The creme de la what? I'm just preparing to go live. Have to report about Imran calling off the lockdown.'

'Wait, what? When did that happen?'

'Haven't you heard? Imran called off the lockdown in Islamabad after the Supreme Court decided to hear the Panama case. I'm so glad. The court has once again spared us from another *dharna*.'

It's strange how my life moves from pain to turmoil without any pauses. Personal struggles always find a perilous equivalent in a public scandal. Since when did I become Sonia? I should put this fact into my first column and build on it in subsequent pieces – so the world and I can understand this bizarre trend.

Khirad is right, though. The country has been spared. But the court proceedings will invade our lives and the drama and political vitriol will just never end. I should call Topsy and ask how Bilal – if he's still in the picture – is coping with the news.

3.40 p.m.

'What do you mean Bilal left?' I ask, secretly relieved that their relationship has ended.

'Just an hour ago,' Topsy says with an air of indifference. 'When the Supreme Court stepped in to the picture, Bilal felt that there was hope for the PTI that he had abandoned. He was already upset because last night I suggested we should take a break from each other. So he decided that since I don't need him anymore, he should go back to something that probably does. Oh well, I'll call you later.'

Topsy hangs up with that succinct explanation. I would have stopped her from putting the phone down and distracted her with my story about Hafeez. But there's a time, place and emotional wavelength for everything. I should just enjoy the rest of my ride. I could use a bit of peace after all that's been happening lately.

I look out the window as we zoom past Khadda Market – I can't possibly go home at such a vulnerable point so I've decided to go to Zainab Market and buy myself a new pair of jeans. The sun glitters against the cars and buildings that shift through my line of vision. I let out a sigh and close my eyes to protect myself against the blinding glare of the sun. Mummy is right. I should always travel with sunglasses.

'You still think Bannu is amazing, madam?' a voice rises from the driver's seat.

When I'd booked my Careem, I didn't bother to check the name of the Captain. All I knew was that it was two minutes away from Koel Cafe. When I hear the Captain's voice, I pull out my phone and read the chauffeur's name on the app. I'm immediately transported from a vulnerable and distressed mood to a pleasant state.

'*Arre,* Bakhtu … Bakhtullah Bhai, *aap,*' I say. Even as the car zips past the Saudi Consulate and I realize that I'm still fifteen minutes away from my destination, I am not burdened by the fear and dreadful possibilities of being bludgeoned with an axe. Till he drops me to my destination, Bakhtu Bhai tells me about his life

in Bannu before and after the operation in North
Waziristan.

I listen in earnest and secretly hope to travel to Bannu
– if not to the non-existent beaches then to the IDP
camps – for research purposes. I can write about it in
my new column. The second option seems more likely
because Mummy will have five strokes and a heart attack
if I even suggest the idea to her. As they say, why kill an
old woman when she has the will and capacity to die on
her own?

Fathers and Lovers

29 July 2017

10 p.m.

Sonia's wedding takes place in the garden of a decrepit house near Korangi Road. The tune of an old wedding song and the rhythm of a beating dhol greet Khirad and me as we enter the venue.

As I expected, it has turned out to be one of those dull monsoon weddings. Earlier today, when I called Sonia to tell her about the weather advisory for the evening, Chhoti Apa answered the phone and insisted that the rain was an outcome of Sonia's habit of eating straight from the cooking pot.

According to Sonia's maid, men and women who dipped their fingers into *deg*s, instead of eating with cutlery and plates, were destined to endure heavy rain on their wedding days. It was a sign from the heavens that god and his angels did not approve of bad table manners.

'*Sonia toh hamesha khati hai deg mein,*' she says, laughing at the sheer absurdity of her own joke. I've seen

Sonia always eating from pots and pans, like Choti Apa says, but it's amusing to think her eating habits can cause as much rainfall as her dramatic tears.

The rain is a big dampener for the wedding. Much as I enjoyed Mira Nair's film where bejewelled women were seen dancing in the rain during a wedding, I don't relish the idea of getting drenched in my sea-green sari with Mummy's fineries dangling from my ears. Sonia should have thought about this before tasting korma with a ladle.

'Tanya,' Khirad whispers into my ear as we walk past a posse of overdressed women and children. 'If at any point you want to leave, let me know. We'll go grab some chai.'

Khirad has insisted on escorting me to the wedding for moral support. She's also here to ensure that I don't end up slaughtering the bride for her enthusiasm or killing the groom for winking at me like he did at the engagement party at Boat Club three months ago. At the time, I was tempted to drag him to Native Jetty Bridge and fling him into the dark ocean like the MQM got rid of all those gunny sacks with bodies in them in Karachi's good old days. But ever since he got engaged, Hafeez has become a lot slyer and a lot less callow than he was before.

'I swear to god, if he tries anything funny with me, I'll ... I'll wring his neck,' I say, struggling to keep my voice low.

'The man will have some nerve to flirt with you on his own wedding day,' Khirad says as she adjusts the hem of her yellow sari. 'That would be so shallow and deceptive.'

As Khirad plonks herself on a chair, Hassan and Bina spot us from a distance and wave. Hassan starts walking towards us and Bina trails behind him like an unwanted pet that has grown too attached to her master. I still don't see why she chose to return to a wily old man like Hassan.

'Don't look now but the high priest of shallow and deceptive is on his way over,' I tell Khirad as I wave back at Hassan. 'You've got to admit, that Hassan has managed to wheedle his way back into Bina's life pretty easily.'

'I guess some things can be forgiven and forgotten,' Khirad says. 'Like cheating on your wife.'

'And how can we forget the cardinal sin of gifting your husband's money to his ex-lover so she can use it for an unpromising business venture?'

Bina races past her husband and hugs me, her nails pressing into my back and her protuberant post-baby belly pressing against my waist as if to push me against the floor.

'Tanya!' Bina chimes excitedly. 'I haven't seen you in such a long time.'

Khirad has turned away so Bina does not acknowledge her presence.

'Yes, Bina,' Hassan says. 'Tanya has been doing some exciting things. She's writing a column for an Indian newspaper and is quite popular. I think she should write a column for the *Daily Image* as well. Why should we be deprived of the country's next Moni Mohsin?'

I force myself to smile. I would never write anything for this sleazeball or his newspaper. No measure of persuasion can make me stoop so low, not even if he offered me a hefty pay package.

Hassan walks over to Khirad. He stands there for a second or two, expecting her to rise from her chair and greet him. She fidgets with the keys on her phone, visibly unperturbed by his presence. He put his hand on her head, ruffles her hair and ruins the blow-dry we got together at Nabila's salon.

'Good to see you,' he says. 'I'm also impressed by the work you're doing lately.'

Khirad looks up from her phone and smiles involuntarily. I can tell that she isn't pleased by the fact that he has spoiled her hair.

'Thank you, sir,' she says, still seated on the chair. 'You were always like a father to me. Your kind words mean a lot.'

Bina shuffles closer towards her husband with territorial ease and grins contentedly. She looked relieved by Khirad's attempt to daddy-zone her husband. For the very first time, I see a smile plastered on Bina Hassan's painted, heavily botoxed face. Hassan's face is painted quite the opposite, with a frown. He nods at us and disappears.

'Well played,' I tell Khirad as Bina also walks away to meet other guests.

Khirad runs a finger through her hair, as if to salvage what she can of her side chignon.

'I figured that since I'm here to make sure that shallow beast doesn't lurk around you, I may as well fight my own shallow beasts along the way.'

Khirad is a quick learner. She'll definitely be going places.

11 p.m.

After the *nikah*, I escort Sonia – who looks stunning in a red trousseau and quite unlike her usual self – to a small room in the house to freshen up and adjust her bridal churidar.

'I can't believe it's happened,' she says. 'I'm finally married!'

'I'm glad it all worked out,' I say, smiling indulgently and lighting myself a cigarette. 'You deserve it.'

'Thanks for being there with me every step of the way.' Sonia holds my hands in her cold, hennaed palms. 'You've been a pillar of support.'

'Don't be silly, Sonia,' I say, struggling to pull my hands away from her as her fingernails pierce into my skin. 'I'm just glad you're happy. Hafeez is lucky to have you.'

She turns away and stares at her reflection in the mirror. Relieved to be free from the prison of her fingers, I walk out of the room and look through my phone and check my messages. That's when I see Hafeez's message of just a few minutes ago.

'Come to the front door of the house,' it reads.

Khirad has warned me against entertaining such requests from the groom.

'He's been doing this to you since the engagement party,' she told me during the Careem ride here. 'Aren't you tired of all the late-night calls and messages?'

I am. But I wouldn't mind meeting him. Khirad doesn't need to know about it.

With curiosity, I skulk out of the corridor to the front of the house and see a sherwani-clad Hafeez standing next to an open window that looks out on to the venue.

'I'm glad you came,' he says when I reach him.

'Congratulations!' I gently pat his shoulder to establish a friendly intimacy between us. 'I'm sure you'll keep Sonia happy.'

A smile creases his face and accentuates his dimples. Hafeez moves closer and tries to draw me into an embrace. I pull away from him. What is it with this husband-wife duo? One wants to prick me with her fingers while the other insists on hugging me inappropriately. God, I wonder what kind of sex they'll have if they continue with these antics.

'I guess you should go,' I say, turning to go back towards the room where Sonia is still adjusting her hair-do and touching up her face. 'You have so many guests to attend to and I need to bring Sonia back on stage.'

Hafeez's face sags with disappointment. He takes a step backwards, shoots one last glance at me and silently walks back to the venue. I lean against the windowpane and watch as he immerses himself into the crowd and steadily blends into it until I can no longer see him.

30 July 2017

12 a.m.

The wrought-iron gates of my house have been thrown open when I return from the wedding. I barely notice it.

My mind is buzzing with a checklist of things I need to do before I fly out to Phuket tomorrow for a much-deserved, long overdue vacation from my city and its eccentric beasts. I haven't even submitted my column to Inder yet.

As I shut the gate, my phone rings. I lean against the parapet and answer the call.

'Hi babe,' Topsy's drunken voice brings a smile to my face. 'How was tonight? Did that creep try anything funny?'

'I pulled away before he could,' I whisper in case my voice travels to the neighbour's house. 'I've decided to let it go. As it is, there's so much more to do. I haven't sent Inder my column.'

'Ah, I sense a blossoming romance there.'

'Don't get too excited. He's seeing someone. Plus, we've kept things strictly professional.'

'That's what they all say.'

'I'm serious. All we discuss is what my next piece should be about. Which reminds me, I should send him my piece before he uses the delay as leverage and makes me write something boring on the JIT report and the Panama verdict.'

'Bilal messaged me, by the way!' Topsy exclaims in a manner that makes a surprise telephone call from her estranged ex-lover sound like the most commonplace occurrence.

After the Supreme Court tossed Nawaz out of the PM House yesterday, the Insafians have been clogging my Facebook newsfeed and Twitter with congratulatory messages. I'm getting sick of their optimism and their told-you-so, holier-than-thou demeanour. I wonder how Bilal would have reacted to the news.

'The message said, "I'm glad I didn't listen to you,"' Topsy laughs. 'Bilal said his Panama verdict has come.'

'I love how he still thinks that he has a role to play in the whole *hungama*,' I say.

Topsy – who has spent the months after Bilal's exit from her life in political isolation and at her sexual zenith – seems to be more at ease now.

'You don't need him anymore,' I continue. 'You're much too busy wooing men and fighting battles in the courtroom.'

'Yeah,' Topsy's lacklustre response reminds me of the long months of sadness that followed Bilal's painful departure from her life. She may have drowned her sorrows in coquetry, but her life is still veiled in unbearable agony. At times, she finds herself tearful and distraught as the deep sadness of the past returns to haunt her. But Topsy has learnt how to dilute her pain. She has started to lead the reticent life she was comfortable with before she met Bilal.

'Let's meet when I return,' I say. 'I haven't seen you since Adam moved to New York last week. It's sad how everyone is moving away or getting married.'

'Yes, Karachi has become quite a lonely place,' Topsy replies softly.

'It's okay,' I assure her. 'When I'm back, we'll make it the city that it should be.'

12.15 a.m.

Mummy is lying on the sofa with her feet propped up against its arm. Tears flow down her face and moisten the heavy layer of rouge she wears on her cheeks.

'Why is the gate open, Mummy?' I ask. 'What's wrong?'

'Daddy was here,' she says, rising from the sofa and clumsily smudging her mascara with her tears.

'What? Why did he come to see you so late?' I pour a glass of water for myself.

'He just wanted to check up on us,' her voice cracks as fresh tears roll down her cheeks. 'He'd heard that you are going to Phuket tomorrow. So he thought he'd say bye.'

'The least he could have done was close the front gate properly,' I say, sipping water from an old mug – no one does the dishes whenever Lurch goes on his leave every two months. 'Things aren't exactly safe, you know. But why are you crying?'

'It's just that...' Mummy struggles to speak. 'I just remembered how alone we really are after he left.'

Mummy always finds a way to stoke drama when it isn't required. Maybe it's finally time to send her to the asylum.

'We've always been alone, Mummy,' I say, wiping her tears with my cold hands, like the good daughter that I'm not. 'But it's better this way.'

'What nonsense!' she sniffs into a handkerchief. 'How is it better?'

I hook my arms tightly around Mummy and kiss her forehead.

'Well, if I were to be honest, Daddy wouldn't understand our banter,' I smile. 'As it is, there's too much estrogen in this house for his liking. Even the cook doesn't seem to have any balls in front of you. Daddy's better off with that *maasi*. And, whether I like it or not, we're better off together.'

Mummy wipes her face and breathes noisily.

'Enough moping about, Mummy.' I dislodge myself from her embrace with an abrupt jerk. 'You need to help me pack. I'm just sending Inder my column before that.'

'Why must you insist on writing these columns?' Mummy's tears reappear on her face. 'Don't you realize that the establishment will come get you for writing columns in India?'

'Don't start with me again, Mummy,' my voice turns into a whimper. 'Why would they care about a Pakistani journalist who writes about the flaws of the people of her class? What's the worst I can do? Let out a family secret about your affair with Lurch?'

Mummy giggles, as if there were a hint of truth to what I said.

'Don't be so *badtameez*,' she taps her palm against my forehead. 'Now go do your work and take out your suitcase. I'll be with you soon.'

As I climb the stairs, I watch from the handrails as the frown on Mummy's face subsides and a broad, beatific smile takes its place. If she weren't wearing so much rouge, she'd look less clownish and more like the fearless woman who brought me up.

'Tanya!' she yells as I enter my room. 'Don't forget to book your Careem for the airport.'

'Yes, Mummy,' I shout back, delighted that she's finally let go of one of her assorted fears – even if it is the most trivial one.

Silence returns to our home – a better houseguest than anyone who has ever visited us. I switch on my laptop, put a cigarette between my lips and touch a lighter against its tip. Between drags, my fingers drum against

the keyboard and raise a gentle clatter that soothes me.
I type keenly and, as I write the final sentence, a halo of
smoke surrounds me, dancing over my head like a ghost.
Its scent clings to my shirt and stays with me until I leave
the room.

Author's note

A few clarifications must be made for readers who aren't familiar with the spaces in Karachi that Tanya visits and the strands of Pakistani politics that have been weaved into the narrative. I have tried to identify a few of these localities on the basis of their geography. Some political references have also been explained:

Abdullah Shah Ghazi's Mausoleum: The tomb of a Muslim mystic and Sufi saint

Agha's Supermarket: A high-end supermarket situated in Clifton

Arts Council: The Karachi Arts Council, a cultural centre in Saddar that promotes music, theatre and fine art

Bandar Park: A recreational park in Orangi Town

Burns Road: Karachi's oldest food street

Cinepax at Ocean Mall: A cinema in Clifton Block 9

Cafe Flo: A restaurant in Clifton Block 4

Chai Wala: A roadside tea establishment on Khayaban-e-Bukhari

Clifton: An affluent neighbourhood in the city

CNIC: Computerized National Identity Card

Defence: A neighbourhood within Clifton Cantonment. It is also known as Defence Housing Authority or DHA. Khayaban-e-Bukhari, Khayaben-e-Ittehad, Khayaban-e-Shahbaz and Khayaban-e-Shaheen fall under DHA.

Dera: A restaurant near Boat Basin

Do Darya: This is an oddly named locality since there are no rivers in the area. Instead there's a cluster of restaurants along the Arabian Sea.

Dolmen Mall: A mall that is situated in Clifton

E Street: A road in Clifton Block-IV

Edhi Home: A charitable venture that was set up by respected philanthropist Abdul Sattar Edhi

Ensemble: A clothing brand in Karachi

Fuchsia: A restaurant on Zamzama that offers Thai cuisine

Ghaffar Kabab House: A barbeque joint in PECHS

Gulgee paintings: Art by Pakistan painter Ismail Gulgee

Hanifia: A restaurant in Boat Basin

Insafians: A term used to describe PTI members or supporters

Johar Mor: The name of a bridge in Gulistan-e-Johar

K-Electric: Karachi's power supply company

Kala Pul: A locality that was named after a *kala pul* (black bridge) that existed in the area. Although the bridge has been replaced with a concrete structure, the name remains unchanged

Keamari: A coastal town in the city

Khadda Market: A market in DHA

Koel Cafe: A restaurant in Block-IV, Clifton

Lal Qila restaurant: An eatery on Shahrah-e-Faisal

Landhi: A large industrial town in the eastern part of Karachi

Liaquatabad: A locality surrounded by commercial zones, which is also known as Lallu Khait

Mauripur: A neighbourhood in Keamari

Mews Cafe: A restaurant on E Street

Muttahida Qaumi Movement or MQM: A political party that maintained control over Karachi

Mohatta Palace: A museum situated in Clifton

Nabila's salon: A beauty parlour owned by Nabila, a renowned hair and makeup stylist

NAPA: National Academy of Performing Arts, a performing arts school on M.R. Kiyani Road

Nueplex Cinema: A cinema in DHA, Phase VIII

PAF Museum: An Air Force museum on Shahrah-e-Faisal

PECHS: Pakistan Employees Cooperative Housing Society, a neighbourhood in Jamshed Town

PTI: Pakistan Tehreek-e-Insaf, a political party that is headed by former cricketer Imran Khan

PTV: Pakistan Television Corporation

PML-N: Pakistan Muslim League, a political party that was led by Nawaz Sharif until February 2018

Qayyumabad Chowrangi: A suburb of Korangi Town

Saddar Bazaar: The main market in the city's cantonment

Sakura: A Japanese restaurant at the Pearl Continental Hotel

Sana Safinaz: A clothing and accessories retailer in the country

Seaview Beach: An accessible picnic point that borders the Arabian Sea

SZABIST: Shaheed Zulfikar Ali Bhutto Institute of Science and Technology

Shahrah-e-Faisal: A major road in Karachi

Sind Club: The oldest club in Karachi, which does not allow membership to women

South City Hospital: A private hospital in Block-III, Clifton

Sultan Masjid: A famous mosque in DHA

Sunset Boulevard: A major thoroughfare in DHA, Phase II,

Tando Allahyar: A small town in the province of Sindh

T2F: The Second Floor, a gallery and cafe established by the late Sabeen Mahmud

Zamzama: Zamzama Boulevard is a bustling street in DHA, Phase V where a large number of designer outlets and restaurants are situated

Zainab Market: Clothing and wholesale market located in the heart of the city

Acknowledgements

I wish to place on record my deep gratitude to Kanishka Gupta, agent and stellar poet, who read the first few drafts of *Typically Tanya* and seamlessly found the novel a home. I would also like to thank Swati Daftuar, commissioning editor at HarperCollins India, for taking a liking to the snide and sharply critical protagonist of this book. Swati's suggestions and unstinted enthusiasm have made this a better book.

Sidhra and Talha, my siblings, listened to endless updates about the book and never flagged in their encouragement. I'd like to thank my childhood friends Abbas Lotia and Eman Malik, who helped me explore Karachi as an adult.

Natasha Japanwala saw Tanya at her mischievous and subversive best. I am eternally grateful to her for not axing her to death. A big shout out to Zebunnisa Burki and Aimen Siddiqui for turning a blind eye as I secretly worked on the manuscript between editing stories. I'd like to thank Halima Mansoor, Zahida, Yusra Hayat, Ali Raj, Yusra Jabeen and Ferdy for all those newsroom interactions that helped me conceive a character like Tanya. I am indebted to Zeba Jawaid, Kamal Siddiqi and Bhaskar Roy for taking a chance on me when no one else would.